FLOATING IN THE NEVERSINK

A NOVEL-IN-STORIES

ANDREA SIMON

Black Rose Writing | Texas

ISBN: 978-1-68433-349-3
PUBLISHED BY BLACK ROSE WRITING
www.blackrosewriting.com

Printed in the United States of America
Suggested Retail Price (SRP) $17.95

Floating in the Neversink is printed in Calluna

"The Attic" won the 2013 Stark Short Fiction Prize; "Tutti Frutti for Me" was published in *New Ohio Review*, Fall 2014.

"Whatever Will Be, Will Be (Que Sera, Sera)" by Ray Evans
© 1955 St. Angelo Music ASCAP admin. by Wixen Music Publishing, Inc.
All Rights Reserved. Used by Permission.

Cover photograph by Andrea Simon
Cover design by Kevin Beard

PRAISE FOR
FLOATING IN THE
NEVERSINK

"Her keen observations are those of a Jewish teen coming of age.... This novel too has its dark edges, as Simon explores complexities of friendship and family."

—*The New York Jewish Week*

"The interconnected stories of *Floating in the Neversink* at first glance seem to portray the innocence of an idyllic past, but soon frays at the edges with its deep secrets, Amanda's unreciprocated love for her father and desire for his approval, even the darkness of sexual violation. In this novel, Andrea Simon captures the loveliness and loneliness of Amanda's youth, and how she comes to terms with the contradictions of her childhood."

—Michelle Cameron, author of
The Fruit of Her Hands and *Beyond the Ghetto Gates*

"The narrator of this humorous and poignant collection of linked short stories is Amanda Gerber, a lively and inquisitive Jewish girl, growing up in the 1950s. Mandy divides her time between a predominantly Catholic neighborhood in Brooklyn, and a Jewish summer community in New York's Catskill Mountains where she's surrounded by her large, multi-generational family.... In her beautiful, descriptive prose, Andrea Simon captures not only the experiences of a childhood but paints a portrait of an entire culture. Here is a broad human seriocomedy flavored with cheese blintzes and vanilla egg creams."

—Katherine Kirkpatrick, author of
The Snow Baby and *Mysterious Bones*

"I laughed and cried at these vivid stories of a girl's Catskills summers and Brooklyn school days as she ages from 9 to 15, from 1955-1961. Adventurous, dauntless Mandy, with her shyer cousin at her side, navigates the inexplicable world of her family with canny observations and a sense of survival. The adults are mired in fading jobs, their real gifts lost in the grind of living and their unspoken secrets: uncles died young, a neighbor's perversity, job loss, infidelity, near drowning, and mental instability. Through all of this, curious Mandy shapes her own world in the woods, in grandmothers' card games, and shut-away rooms. *Floating in the Neversink* is a joy to read."

—Stephanie Cowell, author of
Claude and Camille and *Marrying Mozart*
American Book Award winner

OTHER BOOKS BY
ANDREA SIMON

– Memoir/History –

Bashert: A Granddaughter's Holocaust Quest

– Historical Fiction –

Esfir Is Alive

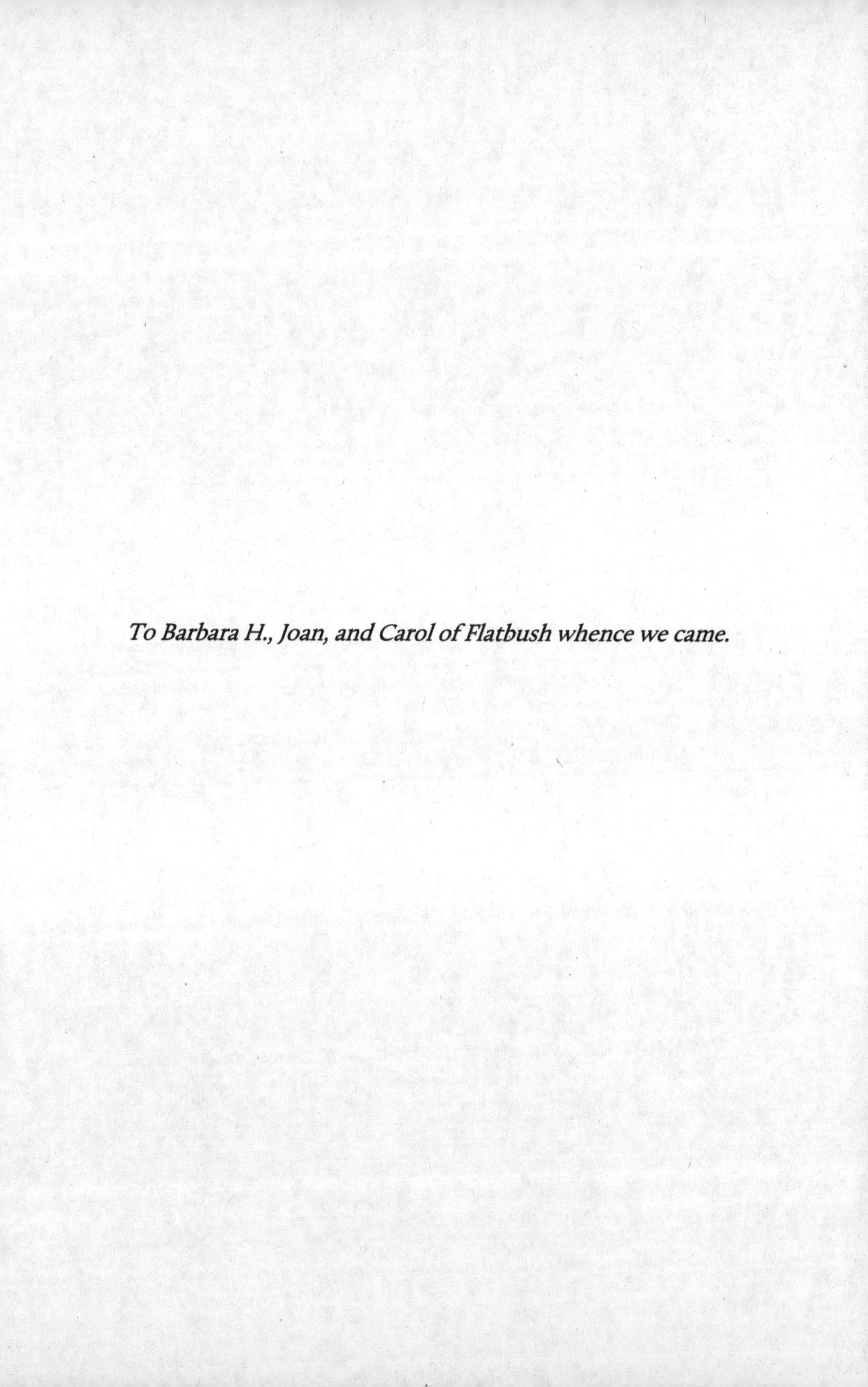

To Barbara H., Joan, and Carol of Flatbush whence we came.

FLOATING IN THE NEVERSINK

CONTENTS

THE RUBBER HAMMER

As my father's new black 1955 Buick sedan quickened down our dead-end street in Brooklyn, on the last Friday in June when I was nine, I cranked my head out the window, straining for a last peek at my best friend, Francine. Just before we turned the corner, I glimpsed a flash of the parochial school's maroon skirts sashaying closer to Francine. I wouldn't be surprised if those girls had been waiting for me to leave before they came in for the kill. I wouldn't be surprised if they were licking twin cherry ice pops, which our nonreligious Jewish mothers forbade for some unexplained reason, just to tempt Francine with an unlicked half.

My mother must have been reading my mind. She said, "Francine's mother is on the invitation committee for the block party this Sunday. She made a special effort to invite the non-Jewish families."

"Really?" I asked. "Francine mentioned it, but I didn't think it would be a big deal."

"Oh, yeah," my mother said. "There'll be a band, children's rides, and all kinds of food. I hear *everyone* is going."

Just ten minutes earlier when I was anticipating a whole summer in the country with my cousin Laura, I got so excited, I jump-stepped upstairs for another false "pee" stop. But now, I didn't want to leave. All I could focus on was Francine's shrinking waving arm, and I didn't want the car to advance one inch past East 22nd Street.

For a while, it was quiet in the car, except for my father now and then screaming, "idiot," "jerk," "stupid," and a few real curse words, to the other drivers on the road. Under a subway el, somewhere downtown, my father said, "Hey, there's H.O. Ward."

"Who's that?" I asked from the back seat. "Is it like H.O. Farina?"

My father laughed and said, "Mandy, read the sign, dummy."

I looked at the large store on the corner, holding back the tears that always came when my father called me dummy. It said, H-O-W-A-R-D Shoes. "Very funny," I said.

"I knew that," my sister, Brenda, said. Sitting next to me, she flipped through her Archie comic book.

"Is there anything you don't know?" I asked her.

"Not really."

"What does that sign mean?" I asked. "It says linger-ee."

"Linger-ee! Can you believe that?" Brenda slapped her knees, laughing like a hyena. "She doesn't even know lawn-jerr-ay when she sees it."

"Maybe you weren't so smart when you were nine," my mother said.

"I always knew how to say it right."

"Brenda, try to act like the thirteen-year-old girl you should be," my mother said.

"I always do," Brenda said in that snotty, Miss Know-it-All voice of hers. "See if you can get this," she said, "How do you pronounce M-A-C?" She spelled each letter separately.

"Mack!" we all yelled.

"How do you pronounce M-A-C-K?"

"Mack!"

"And, how do you say M-A-C-K-E-N-S-I-E?"

"MacKensie," my mother said.

"And, M-A-C-H-I-N-E?"

"I know," I said. "That's Mack-eine."

"I knew she'd get it wrong," Brenda said, hee-hawing all over.

"What, what is it?"

"I don't get it either," my mother said.

"With your brains, I'm not surprised, Estelle," my father said to my mother. My mother gave him what Brenda called her "withering" look.

"Machine, machine, machine," my sister sang.

"Oh, that's cute," my mother said, her voice rising as if she were saying something mean.

•   •   •

When we entered Harlem, traffic got worse, our car stopping and starting with quick jerks. The air was heavy as if we just landed on red Mars without oxygen masks. I rolled down my window all the way and stuck out my head.

"Close that window and lock your door," my father ordered.

"Why? It's so hot," I whined.

"You have to be careful of the *shvartzers*."

"Oh, Bill, must you use that word?" my mother asked.

"What's wrong with it? It means black. They're black, aren't they?"

"It's coarse, that's why. They like to call themselves Negroes."

"So, that means black, too . . . hurry close your window! We're passing a hydrant."

This time, I listened to my father because up ahead a lot of kids—skinny, bare-chested boys wearing shorts, and girls with their skimpy, see-through tops, stuck to their skin by water—crowded around a fire hydrant, while a boy inside the group twisted the huge screw warning everyone to back away. We drove down the street just as the water burst forth in a thick, powerful gush. Someone must have cupped the spout because a showering spray jetted up and across the street, smothering our car in a blinding waterfall. My father braked until the windshield cleared, and said, "Well, the car needed a good wash anyway."

I smiled, happy and relieved that something at least had pleased him.

Just then, the car lurched forward, and I felt a huge thud from behind, thrusting my forehead against the back of the driver's seat. Brenda rolled on the floor, and I heard my mother scream, "Oh no."

"Shit," my father yelled, slamming on the brake.

The next moment, he shoved open his door and fell backward from a whoosh of water.

"Close the door," my mother shouted. "Girls are you alright?" she asked craning her head behind her.

"I guess so," we both said.

My father turned the key and pumped the gas, but the car was stuck. He opened the window a crack and yelled, "Turn the damn hydrant off." The water continued to pour over the driver's side, and we were getting sprayed in the back seat. There was a pounding outside the passenger door, and a man asked if we were okay. He was getting help, he assured us.

Eventually, the water stopped flowing, and two men helped my father push our car forward. From outside, I heard my father and a man screaming, each accusing the other of being blind. The other driver, a man in his 70s, had crashed into our rear bumper and we got stuck in a pothole. Luckily, no one was hurt except for a few feelings.

"That *alter cocker* shouldn't be allowed to drive," my father said once we were moving.

"He probably couldn't see with all that water," I said, feeling the need to defend someone I didn't know, especially an elderly person—and a Negro.

We drove farther uptown, and the hydrant water on the windshield quickly evaporated like the looseness of a sunny-side-up egg hissing and whitening in a frying pan. I rolled down the window again, letting in the fumes of distant rotten garbage and engine exhausts. I watched old women fanning themselves, sitting on stoops; girls jumping double-dutch; hunched men poking into trash cans along the sides of chalk-marked buildings. Spanish store signs; Broadway city buses; the volcanic explosion of occasional fountainheads; and big yellow, bumblebee taxis with black rate signs danced past my window like a Saturday morning cartoon.

Francine was probably still hanging out on my block. I couldn't wait to write her about our accident, how we almost got swept away by a Harlem torrent. By now, she would be sitting on *her* stoop. Would she be starting her letter to me like she had promised? Would she be bouncing her ball, playing "A my name," circling her leg over "Alice" and "Alabama"? Or would she be running in the street, playing catch with the other girls?

We were going faster now, and the air was cooler. "Are we almost at Red Apple Rest?" I asked, noticing more trees in the distance.

"I don't believe her," Brenda said. "We're not even out of the city yet."

"But how much longer?" I leaned forward, pressing my forehead on the back of the driver's seat, the same spot of the crash.

"You're not going to throw up already!" Brenda said.

"No, I won't," I muttered.

"Amanda, we'll get there when we get there," my mother snapped.

I flinched, thinking my father would turn the car around and say we weren't going to the country after all. I was missing Francine so much that maybe this would be a good thing. But he continued driving, and all talking stopped. I couldn't believe that just a short time before, we had been playing word games. That was one thing about my parents. I never knew if the next word would be a joke or a curse.

• • •

I counted state license plates, but it was boring by myself. My mind drifted back to Francine. I couldn't explain why I worried so much about her. She was a loyal friend. When I returned from the country at the end of each summer, she was happy to see me. We'd make bolster forts in my bedroom, and she'd tell me everything about her summer—how the Dennehy girls offered her Necco wafers or bubble gum, how they let her stroke their calico cat, Penny, and how they said ugly things about me. Maybe this September,

Francine would be tired of coming to my apartment and listening to my parents fighting. Maybe she'd think I bossed her around. Maybe she'd no longer want a best friend, or maybe she'd favor another girl by her side, another girl wearing a crucifix on a silver chain. By the end of the summer, Francine could finally go over to my enemy: the Catholics.

• • • •

Francine and I were the only Jewish kids (not counting Brenda) on our side of the street; most of the others were Catholic. We went to public school— I was going into the fifth grade—while most of the Catholic kids went to parochial school. When I was much younger, I thought their teachers were related since there were many sisters, a few brothers, several fathers, but only one mother and she was superior.

A lot of the Catholic girls had names with Marie in it; there were Marie-Anne, Rose-Marie, and plain Marie. They had shoulder-length, light-brown hair, tied back with green plaid ribbons; and along with their maroon uniforms, they wore mismatched, white-cotton anklets with scruffy penny loafers. The boys had freckles, straight blond hair, chipped front teeth, and wet red lips. At least that's how they looked to me as I spied on them playing in the courtyard from my first-floor apartment window.

Unlike the Catholics who went to church often, we didn't go to Hebrew school or the synagogue except for bar mitzvahs, weddings, and funerals. Though raised in an Orthodox household, my mother defied her relatives every December and set up a collapsible, green plastic Christmas tree. In front of the three-foot-tall evergreen, my mother made her own kind of crèche: Rudolf and his reindeer crew, plus a few tin soldiers, a drumming bear, a miniature Russian doll—surrounding a light-glowing Santa—all perched on a white cotton mound. Francine loved playing with Santa and the soldiers. She said it was almost as good as seeing a real-live tree like the Dennehy's Douglas fir topped with a cut-glass angel.

My mother didn't ignore the Jewish tradition. On top of the TV, a foot-tall menorah overlooked our winter wonderland. It was a magical menorah: sterling silver with a music box in the base. I loved to turn the stubby key on the bottom, which clicked like the innards of a fine old clock; and when the key tightened into my thumb, delicate bell-like notes rushed the sad strains of "*Hatikvah.*" I'd wind it over and over again, tears gathering as the hidden baby bass xylophone lost energy, and I'd picture boatloads of concentration camp victims landing in Palestine and kissing the ground.

I never knew that having a Santa and a Star of David in the same room was unusual until my maternal grandmother, Mashie, visited when I was much younger, just when we were lighting the second night's Chanukah candles.

"What kind of Jew are you?" she accused my mother. "My father would turn over in his grave if he saw this."

"Why should the girls have to feel different from the Catholic girls on the block?" my mother said.

"Because they are different, that's why."

● ● ● ●

The first time I met Francine Nederlander was also the first time I met Marie-Anne and Maureen Dennehy. I was five years old, the same age as Marie-Anne, while Francine was four. The Dennehy sisters were playing jacks on the staircase landing of Francine's apartment house, two buildings away from mine. Francine sat on the steps, watching the game, clapping and shouting every time one of the girls caught the tiny rust-colored rubber ball. As Marie-Anne threw up the ball during "'foursies'" and went to snatch the jacks, she accidentally knocked the ball, rolling it into the street.

"I'll get it for you," Francine said, chasing after the ball.

Walking down the block, I adjusted my Indian-bead belt, which held a yellow plastic screwdriver and a black rubber hammer. I was playing "'fix-it,'" searching the ground for anything broken, and I bumped into Francine.

"Oops," she said. "Sorry."

"Look where you're going!" I said.

Ignoring my nasty tone, Francine said, "Did you see a ball? It's red and little."

"Try the curb. Things always get stuck there."

As Francine crouched to look between the metal grates by the curb's intersection, I bent and hammered her toes.

"Why did you do that?" she asked. "'I didn't do anything to *you*." I'd learn that Francine always put logic before emotion.

"I'm fixing them. They're crooked."

Francine looked at her toes, ready to believe almost anything. But the proof was poor. "But they didn't need straightening . . . oh, there's the ball!" she said, scooping it up and darting back to her building.

Despite being curious about what the girls were doing, I knew better than to go where I wasn't invited. My mother warned me plenty of times. So, I skimmed my tools along the concrete ledge that connected our buildings, pretending I was testing the cracked surface. When I got to Francine's building, I tapped at the black-iron banister rod that slanted down six steep-and-long steps to the below-street-level entranceway. To get a better view of the girls, I climbed up on the ledge, put my left leg over the railing as if riding a horse and slid down. But my leg got stuck in the space between the railing and the side of the building, stopping me short, jerking me back and forth like a scarecrow's torso swaying in the wind.

"Owwee!" I cried.

"She caught her leg!" Francine yelled.

"What did she expect would happen?" Seven-year-old Maureen said.

"Yeah, she's stupid," Marie-Anne said, "dancing around with that boy's belt."

"She didn't mean it," Francine said and climbed up to the step closest to my thigh. She tried to lift it up, but it wouldn't budge. "Can you help?" she asked the sisters, who stood watching.

Finally, Francine reached under my thigh. Marie-Anne and Maureen clasped my ankles, and they heaved.

"It's no use," Francine said. "My daddy told us never to play there. I better get him."

She ran down the block where her father was washing his car. That's how it was in those days; we were on our own, but someone's parent was nearby, or we could yell, and heads would pop out of the window.

As we waited for Francine's father, I felt open scrapes burning along my leg and a throbbing tightness clutching my heel to the banister end. Recently, I overheard my grandmother describing European Jews stuck on a staircase to death. Would this happen to me?

I dreaded what Mr. Nederlander would say, but all he wanted to know was if I could move my leg and where it hurt. It took him no time to lift me out of the space, and as I stood, he circled a rapidly forming bump on my ankle and told me that he would carry me home so my mother could wrap it with a cold compress.

"Does it hurt a lot?" Francine asked as she trotted alongside.

"It's not so bad," I lied. "But I'm sorry that I hammered your toes."

"Oh, that's okay."

I figured if Francine could forgive me for hammering her toes and swallow her pride and call her father to rescue me, and if she could stand up to the Dennehy girls just to help *me,* she would be my best friend and true sister for life. All I had to do was make sure no one took her away from me.

• • •

Remembering this got me even more nervous. Brenda mentioned that it would be about a half hour until we reached the Red Apple Rest, our halfway stop. Finally, my father steered the car into the exit ramp, and I could see the restaurant's massive white building with the striped overhang and the big red apple on the roof.

"I'm going for gas," my father said. "Don't get lost."

"We'll get seats inside," my mother said to my father, as we Gerber females automatically hurried to the restroom. Waiting on line, my mother said, "Mrs. Dennehy told me they were renting a cottage at Brighton Beach for a week this summer."

"Really?" I said with a battering heart.

"Yes, Francine's mother apparently gave her the name of a relative who had empty rooms."

The Nederlanders always rented lockers at Brighton Beach Baths. Now the Dennehys and the Nederlanders could join hands in the saltwater pool or skip waves in the Atlantic Ocean. Maureen and Marie-Anne and Francine could undress in adjoining lockers. They could play ping pong and visit that booth in Coney Island where Francine and I made a record pretending to be Rosemary Clooney and Vera-Ellen singing "Sisters." I couldn't stand the thought.

"Mommy," I asked, "How long would it take to turn around and drive back to Brooklyn?"

"Now you want to go back, after all the weeks of pestering me about going to the country? I thought you couldn't wait to see Laura. I'll never understand you, Mandy."

I shrugged, deciding to write Francine the minute I got to Mountainview. I would give the letter to my father, begging him to slip it under her door right after he parked the car on East 22nd Street on Sunday night. I would draw pictures of our car stuck under the Harlem downpour. I would remind Francine of her visit in August, listing new adventures we'd have in the country. There wasn't a moment to lose, not if Francine would be swimming in the same waters as the Catholic girls.

A HORIZONTAL WEED ON A COUNTRY ROAD

No matter how I memorized things like yards and where the sun sets and lines on maps, I never understood how anyone got anywhere. If someone told me to go east three-hundred feet or to follow the line parallel to Flatbush Avenue for twenty minutes, I'd be as lost as a blind camel in a desert. But I knew one thing for sure like it came to me in a dream or was put under my pillow for me to know by heart when I woke. I knew what a mile meant. I knew how long it took to drive a mile, walk a mile, run a mile, and where to stop for rests along a mile road. I knew that a mile was a long time to get to where you wanted, but just long enough to be worth the time spent getting there. Waiting the length of a mile was about all the suspense I could hold in without exploding. I knew this because it was exactly one mile from the beginning of River Road, leading from the village of Mountainview, to our A-frame cottage in the country. The country where I roamed half-naked with my hand-carved bow and arrow. The country where knobby, beckoning fingers camouflaged between thatched berry bushes.

My father had driven a hundred miles from Brooklyn's Grand Army Plaza to our Catskill Mountain village square, down a hill, past all the familiar jammed arrows and signs: Shady Grove Hotel, Kosher; Woodville Bungalow Colony, Pool; Neversink Lodge, 1¾ miles. The first building on the right side of River Road was the laundry—a cavernous redbrick building where the hotels sent their sheets, towels, and tablecloths. The other side of the road was uninhabited with tall weeds hiding railroad tracks, following the path two miles past my house, as far as the Neversink River.

"Hurry get down!" my father shouted as we approached Woodville Bungalow Colony.

I ducked on the floor, pinched my nose, and held my breath.

"It's safe now," my father said, driving a short distance farther.

"Germs can find a person even in the back seat," my sister said.

"I know," I said, though no one could convince me since a boy died of polio there three summers before.

We passed the Shady Grove Hotel's group of white semi-attached cabins, Bavarian brown-beamed main house, long shuffleboard court, where more people sat and played cards than played shuffleboard, and L-shaped pool, where Brenda hung out with a lifeguard named Bruce Reiger, who I suspected was her boyfriend last summer though God forbid she would tell me, her lowly little sister. Shady Grove blended into Ratner's, fifteen similar-looking, white wood bungalows and a large white ranch house on the far end, where Mr. and Mrs. Ratner lived with their six dogs—reddish-black attack animals with ugly crimson, foaming mouths and pointy vampire teeth.

The same way that it was hard to tell where Shady Grove left off, and Ratner's began, it was hard to know where Ratner's ended, and our land started. One driveway separated us. Our house, actually my grandma Sarah's, was compact and brown-shingled, with an arched, elaborately carved floral wooden front door opened through brass circle handles. Its red-stone porch ledges displayed an array of A-frame replica birdhouses; and a seemingly identical small-stoned, sculptured pedestal-sink birdbath sentineled each side of the front lawn. Everything had been lovingly constructed by Sarah's husband, Sam, my grandfather, who died of a sudden heart attack before I was born. He had a fondness for birds of all kinds.

"We're here! We're here!" I yelled so loudly that I was sure the guests at Shady Grove heard me while sipping their glasses of tea in the dining room.

Swerving to avoid the driveway's chunks of broken pavement, my father shouted, "Goddammit to hell! This is worse than ever. When are the Ratners going to stop driving their dilapidated truck on our property?" He stopped at the garage door, and the Ratner dogs barked like crazy.

"Here they go again. Another summer with those howling monsters. I have a good mind to poison them all this year," my mother hissed, vigorously shaking her head back and forth.

"Mommy, please, you wouldn't!" I said.

"What do you think, dummy?" Brenda asked.

We weren't out of the car for a minute when a screeching, staccato metallic sound came from the PA System: "Attention. Testing. Testing. Is it working? Oh, it's on? This is Sophie, your social director here at Shady Grove, your home away from home. Ladies and gents, tonight I'm happy to report we have *quite a program* for you. Melvin, the head waiter, will sing a few folk songs for your listening enjoyment. Canasta and bridge tables will be set up in the casino, and Rabbi Bornstein will talk about planting trees in Israel at the lawn chairs by the pool. Don't forget, tomorrow after breakfast,

Flossie will teach calisthenics on the shuffleboard court, followed by an exciting game of Simon Sez. Don't miss it."

"Quite a program!" my father said, his hands squeezing the steering wheel. "Quite *A* program."

•　　•　　•

The next morning, after Flossie announced her class, I heard my father yell, "Hey Leon, you old bum." My heart sank. I suddenly forgot my day's plans of picnicking and fishing at the Neversink River and wished that we were back on East 22nd Street in our cramped tenement apartment. My mother, who didn't speak to anyone before three cups of coffee, rushed outside. I could understand why my father sounded excited to see Leon. They grew up together and were associates in the sweater business, but I couldn't understand what my beautiful and sophisticated mother saw in the ugliest man in the world.

Tall and heavy, Leon had a thin black mustache. His part—a line of pink skin—began over his right ear and then five or six strands of pasted-down brown-gray hair swept all the way up and over to the other side of his head, ending in little greasy arrowheads. Leon's cheeks were puffy and flushed, and he had tiny red lines on his nose like river marks on a map. He popped pellets of Sen-Sen into his mouth with the frequency of a machine gun; somewhere he had read that this breath freshener was used by movie stars.

"Girls, come out and say hello to Leon," my mother called.

Squashed against the kitchen's screen door, Brenda gave me an eye roll, and I returned it with a giant nod. We joined the adults who were now sitting in the green Adirondack chairs on the lawn.

"How long are you staying this year?" my father asked Leon.

"Naomi is in Florida with her mother and will join me Wednesday. Then another week here."

Every summer that I remembered, Leon and his wife spent two weeks at the Shady Grove Hotel while their sons were at camp. And every summer, I pretended I was sick if my father was going to visit him. When Leon appeared, I fled to my room.

"Come here," Leon said, waving to me. "Let's have a look at you." He held me at arm's length. "M'mm still skinny, but you have your mother's long sexy legs. You'll be something all the boys will go after." Then he winked and patted his knee. "Sit on Uncle Leon's lap."

I inched toward him, praying over and over to myself, "God, please don't let Leon say or do anything, please God, if you're really there."

I stood facing Leon, and he turned me around and lifted me on his knees, holding me around my waist and pumping his legs as if I were a crying baby. Taking out photos of his sons tucked in his shirt pocket, Leon passed them to my mother. Then he placed his palms on my shoulders and rubbed my back up and down. "No bra yet, kiddo?" he whispered in my ear.

"What?"

"Too young I guess for a titslinger, sexy?"

Afraid I was going to cry, I didn't answer and shrugged. While my parents passed around the photos, Leon continued talking to me in a very low voice. "Would you like to go berry picking with me again?"

My face flamed and a valve in my throat closed. Though the last time was two years ago, I could still feel Leon's craggy fist clenched over mine, instructing me how to pick a blueberry: "Coddle it. Feel it all around," he had crooned. "All you have to do is give it a slight tug. When it's ripe, it will fall into your hands." I could still see his blue-black finger stains on my white "Saturday" scripted cotton panties. I could still hear his threats, warning me not to tell my parents. They would punish me, even send me to a special jail for girls like me. I couldn't believe Leon was here again. Not again. Not again.

"I remember when you were a toddler. You used to walk all over without any clothes," Leon mumbled.

My mother sashayed to Leon's chair, with a photo in her hand. "Look Leon, doesn't Kevin have the same profile as your mother?"

I squirmed in Leon's lap as he jiggled his knees. "Hey, sit still, mushy tushy," Leon said, this time louder.

"When are you going to stop calling her that?" my mother said in a tone that didn't sound very angry.

Ignoring Leon's remarks, my father went in the house, returning with two bottles of soda, a Coke for him and Leon's favorite, Dr. Brown's Cel-Ray. After a few swigs, Leon pressed his mouth to my ear and gave out a trombone-tuning belch, emitting a sourish combination of celery, licorice, and his breakfast that must have been hard-boiled eggs, and I tasted vomit crawling up my throat.

Brenda appeared in her red polka-dot bathing suit, and I felt Leon pivot his lap in her direction. Then he emitted the longest wolf whistle. Brenda disappeared across the driveway to Ratner's, heading for Shady Grove. She was not going to let Leon ruin her social life.

My mother and Leon gossiped about a new Mozart record, and I half-stood. I inched away and scooted to the other side of the lawn, squatting between two lilac bushes. I sat and stared beyond my father's car in the driveway while blurry images of hairy hands and thumping thighs flashed onto the white flaky garage door, reverberating like movie reels slapping into rewinding spools.

I lost track of time; my next conscious moment found me midway down the driveway, where I turned as if something had forced me to look back. Leon and my parents, now joined by two pinochle-playing men from Shady Grove, were sitting in a circle, whispering and laughing—laughing with open mouths getting bigger and bigger, stretching into giant open pits, howling like the Ratner dogs. Leon stood and faced the driveway, pointing toward me, chanting, "berry picking, berry picking." I swung my head in front of me and then whipped it around again. No one made eye contact with me. I shut my eyes and rubbed them with my fists. When I spied the group again, they were sipping their drinks and smoking as if nothing had happened. I blinked and blinked. Now, the adults were on the grass, sitting stiffly in an Indian powwow, arms folded, staring ahead as if watching a bonfire, spellbound by the crackling orange flames and heavy gray smoke of burning totems.

I ran to the road and drifted in the direction of the Neversink River. I was overcome by a shriveling, faraway feeling. I didn't hear the cars whiz by but could feel their random breezes; I didn't hear the Ratner dogs barking even though the ground rumbled as they jumped and strained against their chains tied to the post behind a nearby shack. On the road, I saw familiar passersby's lips moving, but no one called my name. Then a thought came to me with such force like God shot it down in a bolt of lightning to land right in my head: I just was not like everyone else in this world. There were real breathing people like my parents and Leon, but there was something different about me, something deep within. My cells were not made of the same substances as normal people. Mine could become transparent; I could float through space, watching others, unseen. I was invisible.

Now it all made sense. Last week at a Flatbush delicatessen, the waiter gave a menu to everyone at the table but me. The clerk in the Ditmas Avenue grocery store had asked the woman behind me in line if she was next. My teacher had read the roll book in class for attendance but skipped my name.

As I ambled past an open field, I picked up, chewed, and sucked on the sweet stems of those tall yellow-green weeds with the furry tips. At that moment, I knew that anyone looking for me, Amanda Gerber, would see a long green weed in a horizontal plane, traveling down a country road.

Somehow, I changed direction, but it's hard to tell when until I found myself climbing up my driveway. A thick glob clutched my throat like I ate too much, too quickly. The gummy mass plodded down a windpipe, past two lungs, past one belly. It was as if each organ were taking shape slowly like an exposed print in a developing tray. All I had to do was concentrate on a bodily section, and little by little, I could see legs, arms, fingertips.

Amazingly, I couldn't control these outer forms. I needed something to help me pass again as a real person, be what anyone wanted me to be. I squeezed my eyes as tight as I could, and a little glass bottle appeared in my hand, a little glass bottle only I could see. It contained insides for me to swallow. My lifetime job was to carry this bottle in my hand, to remind me that no matter how good I felt, my true self was empty.

"Mandy!" a woman called. It was my mother.

"Amanda Gerber, what in the world is wrong with you? You're acting like a four-year-old not nine."

My mother's voice drew me closer to them.

"Amanda to earth, do you hear me?"

"I told you I think she should spend less time in the woods with Laura," Leon said.

I didn't have a choice; I couldn't let Leon win. Heading right for the middle of the circle of chairs, I took a swig from the unseen bottle, waited for the magic substance to activate my organs, and said hello to everyone like I was happy to see them.

BLOOD COUSINS

In the past, my cousin Laura and I explored whenever her mother shopped in the village or played mahjong at Siegel's Bungalow Colony. But now that Aunt Virginia had a new baby, there was no telling when she would go away, and I couldn't wait to get to our secret rock, the one we had discovered last summer when I was eight and Laura seven. On this first of July, the day Laura's family arrived, I had a tough job convincing my cousin that her mother wouldn't be on the warpath if we disappeared. But she finally agreed to go the following day on the condition that we ask my sister to tell anyone who might look for us that we had just left our grandma Sarah's house, the place our families shared every summer.

Early the next morning before we heard human stirrings, Laura and I met in the kitchen, gobbled a few bites of a stale onion roll from the red metal roll-top bread bin, and quietly closed the screen door. We ran past the apple trees and across the swing area, not even stopping for our customary first leg pumps of the summer until we reached the wishing well—where the flat land merged into the rocky woods.

We stayed on the left side, closest to Siegel's Bungalow Colony because if we went too far right, we could get stuck in the big boulders behind Ratner's Cottages. Soon, we found the barbed-wire fence and traced it to the spot twisted up in a tangled half-moon, leaving a foot or so of space from the ground. I scrunched on my back and, with my elbows and palms digging into the earth, swept my behind to the side, stirring pebbles and dust like a broom, then poking my head under the raised wire. I was free to stand.

With a stick, I lifted the thorny metal opening a little higher, and Laura crawled under. Once we were both clear, we plucked a few tall yellow-green weeds and skipped up the narrow path, which my father had cut three years ago when he took us berry picking.

Laura and I passed a line of blackberry bushes and followed another path farther up the hill, ending by a large rock (newly named Big Rock) with a smaller rock on each side. A huge oak tree stood behind. It was the tallest tree I had ever seen.

Down another hill and below the Big Rock was a wide, bumpy ledge. We called it the Sun Rock because there were no trees around it and the stones felt very hot. To the side of the Sun Rock was a half-buried tank covered with a black, metal cellar-like door. A plaque read "Siegel's Cesspool." We wanted to know what a cesspool was, but if we asked our parents, they'd wonder where we saw that word.

Just yesterday, I heard Mr. Siegel say something about a cesspool when he spoke to my parents about fixing our well. I listened hard and, from what I could tell, it had something to do with our toilets. The dirty-diaper smell when we stood by that metal tank near the Sun Rock now made sense.

We were so tired from climbing the hill that by the time we got to the Big Rock, we leaned all the way back against the trunk of the oak tree, which was better to sit against than our bolsters or pillows on our beds at home. I flattened my hand on my head like I was measuring myself and ran my fingers upward in a straight line. Over a hard, bumpy bark, I felt a smooth knob about the size of my spread hand. Then I turned. It was still there—Laura's and my name separated by a squiggle. It had taken me hours to carve. Laura turned too, saw my finger pointing to the names, and smiled.

"It's real nice here, isn't it?" I said.

"Yeah," Laura answered in a dreamy voice.

Stretching out on the rock, with our heads resting on our clasped hands, we looked up. All I could see were tall branches of the oak tree, reaching up and up without end. Tiny beams of white-blue light came through spots between the branches. Hundreds of green leaves, getting smaller and more yellowish as I looked higher, twinkled in my eyes like a bouquet of sparklers on the Fourth of July. I couldn't stop blinking in time with the ins and outs of these fake fireflies circling the leaves.

"Look," I said, "you think God is signaling us with a giant light like those S.O.S. flashes boats give each other?"

"Yeah. My daddy says that God tells us when he's bowling."

"How does God do that?" I asked.

"God makes thunder when he gets a strike. When God misses the pins, he cries. And then it rains."

"Grandma Sarah says that it snows when God is cleaning his house. When he fluffs the pillows, the feathers plunge to snowflakes."

"I guess he doesn't clean that much," Laura said.

"Maybe he does most of his cleaning when he's hanging over Alaska."

"But no kidding, Mandy, do you believe there is a real God doing all these things?"

"I don't know, do you?"

"I guess so. Do you ever pray to God?"

"I say my prayers every night, just in case."

"Really? What do you say?"

"I watched Jeff on *Lassie* saying his prayers. My mother taught me the poem about if you die before you wake. But I think that's too scary. So, I just say a mixture like, 'Now I lay me down to sleep. God bless everyone I know, and please God let everything be all right.' This way I don't feel bad for leaving anyone out."

"Sometimes I ask God to let me know he's there."

"I do that, too. I tell him I won't step on the cracks in the sidewalk for two blocks and then he should let a car honk."

"I never told anyone this, Mandy. So, promise, you won't tell."

"I promise."

"Before my mother got Michael, I asked God for a baby sister."

"Why?"

"I don't know. I guess because I heard my daddy say he wanted a boy this time. But we got a boy anyway. Do you think God is punishing me for something?"

"No. Maybe your mom or dad asked for a boy. God can't give everyone their wishes."

"I guess so."

"I wish God would throw us a peanut butter and jelly sandwich. I sure am hungry," I said.

"Me too."

Laura and I looked extra hard at the patch of light, and I had my mouth open just in case. But I knew God was too important to worry about our tummies.

"Let's play John and Jim," I said.

"Okay, but we should get back soon."

"We can make a few arrows for our Indian episode."

Laura didn't answer but followed my lead, letting off little sighs to let me know she would rather be doing anything else, like reading a Casper comic. We found a tiny tree and bent two long twigs back and forth until they snapped off. We lifted a bark sliver by each stem and peeled a long piece, stripping off the bark until the twigs were white and clean, getting bits of green tree residue underneath our nails.

Laura played the part of Jim, and I, her brother, John—two boys who got into lots of trouble like Tom Sawyer and Huck Finn, but who also did good things like Robin Hood. As we worked on our arrows, I suggested we continue our Western adventure, with John and Jim visiting a Cherokee village. "The chief can help the boys make bows from two long branches so that they can accompany the braves to find a scout who was kidnapped by an enemy tribe," I said.

"Let's take a break," Laura said after we gathered larger branches for our bows.

"But we didn't go to the Indian village yet."

"Next time."

I buried the bows and arrows in a pile of leaves near the Big Rock and clambered onto the Sun Rock. I could see the whole country—down the hill into a forest of rounded, green treetops, sprinkled among tan, yellow, and white—flat specks of Siegel's Colony. And, in the distance, way across the country, past all the roads, were the evergreens hanging on the cliffs—the up-and-down tree line of the Catskill Mountains, with the cloudless, bright blue sky on top.

"Laura, come here. The view is great."

"I like it better on our rock. It's shady, and you can see almost the same things if you stand tall."

I stepped back a little and almost tripped on the handle of the cesspool door. Squatting, I found a long branch and stuck it under the handle. Then I rose, pulling on the branch. The door squeaked open. I then clutched the edges of the door and heaved it back so that it rested on its rusty hinges. The stink was worse than when we passed Elizabeth, New Jersey in the car; it practically knocked me out.

"Mandy, what are you doing?" Laura cried. She was standing on our rock. "Close that door quick, before someone comes."

"Nobody is coming. Besides, we can see the path from here."

"Ugh, that's disgusting. Close it, Mandy."

"In a minute," I shouted back. "I just want to have a better look."

I moved a few feet away, to breathe clean air into my lungs, then returned to the opened door and peered inside. The walls were thick and muddy, and I could see murky water below and what appeared like a small ledge on the other side of the pool, which held a notebook. I tried to reach it, but my arms were too short. I slipped off my sandals, flipped over, lay on my stomach, and stretched my toes from behind me until I felt a long cloth spine and a cardboard cover. I tried to grasp the spine with my toes but couldn't get a good grip.

I felt a heavy weight on my leg. The cesspool door fell and was about to crush me. A searing pain pierced my shin. I cried out.

"Help, Laura, the door." My toes didn't move. Panicked and in pain, I began to cry.

Laura scrambled to my side, her hands shielding her eyes, screaming, "Mandy, Mandy."

"You've got to help me, Laura."

"I can't, I can't." Laura was making huffing noises.

What did she mean, she can't? I couldn't believe it. "Get that branch and slide it through the handle and then pull hard," I ordered, gritting my teeth as pain radiated through my leg. This was way worse than getting my foot caught in the banister on East 22nd Street.

Laura stood frozen.

"Laura, remember you're Jim. Do it Jim, just do it!" With my free leg, I pushed the door enough to relieve the pressure from my trapped leg. I finally heard the door thump to the side.

Laura fell as the branch snapped in her hand. "I did it," she said. "I did it." She sat bug-eyed, grasping the broken branch as if it were a bar of gold.

"Jim, help me up," I screamed, afraid she couldn't hear me in her sleepwalking state. I swung my leg around, clutched Laura's arm, and pulled myself off the cesspool. The back and side of my leg were covered with mud, and the shinbone was bumpy and whitish. But at least there was no blood.

We sat silently for several minutes. I kept flexing my foot to see if it worked. It felt stiff and tingly but moved all right.

"I was so scared, so scared. But I helped you!" Laura said in a semi-bragging tone.

"I was scared, too." I didn't think it was time to remind her that if I hadn't yelled for Jim, I could have lost my leg.

Watching me stand, she asked, "How does it feel?"

"A miracle. I think it's okay, considering. I guess God doesn't watch us when it matters," I said.

"What do you think was in that notebook?" Laura asked.

"I wish I knew, but I'm not opening that door again."

We slinked off the Sun Rock, and I circled a small area, testing my foot. Everything seemed normal. Laura tailed me into a wooded area, not far from a bunch of short trees and blueberry bushes, the same ones I went to with Leon. Not wanting to stay there, I turned in the opposite direction back to the Big Rock. A long wailing noise, like the air-raid warning at school, went off.

"That's the siren. It must be noon," Laura said. "We'd better go."

I said. "Laura?"

"What?"

"You saved me. Let's swear to be blood cousins."

"Okay, but what do we have to do?"

I took a bobby pin from my hair, peeled off the rubber tip, and ran the point back and forth on the rock's hard gray surface to make it sharp. I closed my eyes and jabbed the point in the fat part of my pointer fingertip. When I opened my eyes, a little red bubble had formed.

"That's blood!" Laura said, pinching her forehead.

"I know. Now you do it."

"I can't. It'll hurt."

"Not if you do it quick."

"I can't. I'm scared."

"Don't you want to be blood cousins?"

"Yes, but . . . okay, but you do me."

Laura shut her eyes and handed me her finger. I stuck the bobby-pin point in fast.

"Ouch!"

"Come on, it wasn't that bad."

"Now what? I'm not doing anything else with blood!"

"Give me your finger." I placed mine over hers so that both bloody puddles smeared together. "Now, press firmly and repeat after me. 'I John, of John and Jim.' But you say, 'I Jim, of John and Jim.' "

"I Jim, of John and Jim."

"Known in the real world as Mandy and Laura."

"Known in the real world as Mandy and Laura."

"Do solemnly swear that we are blood cousins."

"What is solemnly?"

"Just say it!"

"Do solemnly swear that we are blood cousins."

"For the rest of our lives."

"For the rest of our lives."

"Amen."

"Amen."

I yanked two oak leaves from the tree, handing one to Laura. "Here," I said, "wrap it around your finger like a Band-Aid. By the time we're home, the bleeding will stop."

We climbed off our rock and walked down the path to the barbed-wire fence, every few seconds examining our fingers. I tried to ignore the pulsing ache in my leg.

"Mandy?" Laura asked as we scurried from under the fence.

"What?"

"Do you have any other blood cousins?"

"Of course not! How could you think that?"

"I was just asking, that's all."

I didn't tell Laura, but I was already plotting to steal a hammer and crowbar from my father's toolbox in the garage. Maybe I would take an old tennis racket or a shovel. I didn't know how to make this into another John and Jim adventure, but somehow the boys would return to the cesspool and get that notebook.

My new blood cousin and I skipped past the wishing well. Laura dropped her oak leaf near the swings. I picked it up, folded it into a triangle, and slipped it into the pocket of my shorts, meaning to put it with my leaf in the wood cigar box—the one I hid under the stuff in the attic trunk, the one that kept the things I planned to save for the rest of my life.

GIN RUMMY

About an hour after our fathers left for the city, Grandma Sarah came into the Sun House where Laura and I were gluing toothpicks into rectangles and triangles for a future dollhouse-building project.

"Girls, how about putting your things away and helping me?"

"Helping you do what?" Laura asked.

"Setting up for a game of gin rummy."

That's all she had to say. We sprang into action, sweeping up bits of bent toothpicks and crumbling newspapers we had spread over the trunk that served as the all-purpose Sun House table.

An octagonal, brown-shingled, one-room building near the driveway, about two car lengths from the main house, the Sun House was open with big screens as windows and a screen door. My grandfather Sam had built it so people could sit there when it was too hot and not be bothered by wasps and mosquitoes. I didn't understand why everyone called it a Sun House since its purpose was to get away from the sun.

Inside, there were two overstuffed green-fern chairs, a long matching glider couch that swung on a metal frame, and a folding bridge table and wooden chairs stacked in the corner. The furniture smelled of old cigar smoke and unwashed socks.

Laura and I loved to play there because, depending on where we were inside, we could view everywhere—from the woods in the back to the kitchen door of our house, which our two families shared, from Siegel's Bungalow Colony on the side beyond the pine trees to Ratner's on our other side toward the village of Mountainview. We could see who drove up the driveway and who was hanging clothes on the line strung between two apple trees not far from my grandmother's window.

Like she did on many other country evenings, especially when the men weren't here, Grandma Sarah played cards, she said, "to pass the time." She never admitted that she liked the game, but I could tell she did by the way she fussed about, getting the table and chairs in the perfect spots, putting an ashtray or cup or tissue next to the right person—depending on who was playing that night.

Mainly, Grandma Sarah played with other grandmothers. If my mother or Laura's mom wanted to join, Sarah told her daughters-in-law they had better things to waste their money on. But if my mother's mother, Mashie, was visiting, Sarah would be itching to play. And, if Laura's other grandmother, whose name was Rose, rented a bungalow at Ratner's for two weeks, as she did every summer, then the three grandmas played their special three-player, two-deck version way into the night, each bragging the next morning that her bones were the stiffest and squeakiest.

The three grandmas also competed over their cooking, particularly their pies. We had to be extra careful about what we said when tasting; it was best to just mumble "umm" or "ahh." Grandma Sarah was known for her fresh peach pie, with a perfectly pinched crust and duplicated sugared strips precisely aligned across the top. Rose baked tiny blueberry pies, the size of a hand—too small to pick off a flake without making a big dent. Mashie bragged about her "this and that" apple pie, which never looked like much, but always tasted delicious. If asked what she put in, Mashie never remembered, saying, a "pinch of this" and a "pinch of that."

When the three of them played cards together, Grandma Sarah avoided serving any of their baked pies because she didn't want to start out with bad feelings. On card nights, she bought sweet rolls and marble cake from the bakery in town. And that's how it was this night. With Mashie and Rose having arrived the day before, this would be the first game of the summer.

"Mandaleh, can you get out the pad?" Grandma Sarah asked.

In the coffee-table trunk, she saved brown notebooks with the grandmothers' card scores, going back years. Sometimes, the grandmas let me write down the scores, but that got me nervous because they kept checking my math.

I loved to watch them play, even though I never knew who to root for since one of them was a guest and I wanted to be polite, and the two other players were my grandmothers. When I watched, they tried to get me on their sides, bribing me with a piece of cake or a penny. Usually, I rooted for the one who was losing.

After Laura and I helped Grandma Sarah move the trunk and unfold the card table, we pushed a large crate next to her chair. She needed this extra space to stack her cards in little piles, according to suits or numbers, before she decided what to throw out. On the right side of Mashie's playing area, we put a blue glass ashtray; and, by Rose's table corner, we placed a saucer for her coffee cup.

Since Rose always asked me to pour her a cup, I called her Mrs. Coffee, and it became a joke with us. Whenever we saw each other, I said to her, "Coffee, Mrs. Coffee?" And she answered, "Don't mind if I do, Miss *Kibitzer*." She said it was unusual for a nine-year-old girl to be so interested in a bunch of old ladies. But I knew she liked me hanging around and asking questions; sometimes she put down her cards to remember something from her past. I never got enough of those stories—how all three women came over from Europe on the Boat, lived a lot of years in different places, and then, at certain times in their lives, wound up together in Mountainview, here in the Catskill Mountains.

For eleven years after her husband died, Mrs. Coffee owned a hotel, near a blueberry farm, about three miles past town. She was a big, strong woman and did the cooking and a lot of the work herself, with the help of her two daughters, one being Laura's mother, Virginia, who married my father's brother, Sol.

My grandmother Sarah came to Mountainview to escape work troubles in the family sweater factory in Brooklyn, New York. She and my grandpa Sam put in long hours and contended with a greedy landlord and union bosses. They wanted to build their dream house so they could retire some day and leave their knitting business to my father and Uncle Sol. When Sam died before he retired, his sons got the business anyway.

Mashie, who was tall and beautiful, well, she concocted a very long story of how she got to Mountainview, telling anyone who asked. In a nutshell, when she was in her thirties, she moved her large family to the country because her doctor told her she needed clean mountain air. She bought an old, rundown house in town. My grandfather, Rabbi Herschel, had a hard time making a living since the Jews in Mountainview weren't religious, so Mashie set up a boardinghouse. Herschel was very jealous of the men who rented rooms, and he screamed in the streets about them.

Mashie and Herschel divorced; and Mashie moved back to Brooklyn, where the other two grandmas also lived during the non-summer months. Unlike them, Mashie had a husband—her third (the second died of a head injury), a handsome man named Michel who lived in Germany. Mashie went back and forth to Germany, Brooklyn, and Mountainview, though her visits to Germany were becoming less frequent. I guess it was hard to fit Mashie's story in a tiny nutshell—unless it was more like a coconut.

• • •

Before long, the three grandmothers sat in their seats groaning and tapping the table.

"Coffee, Mrs. Coffee?" I asked Rose.

"Why, I don't mind if I do, Miss *Kibitzer*."

"Can we take your orders, ladies?" Laura asked, turning to an empty sheet from Grandma Sarah's score pad.

"Sure, Lauraleh," Grandma Sarah said. "A glassaleh tea for me and you know how I like it."

"I'll have tea too," Mashie said. "You can use the same tea bag. And, maybe just a little piece of something sweet."

Laura and I went in the house, tied aprons around our waists, and brought in a tray with the orders. We handed Mrs. Coffee her coffee, placed Grandma Sarah's glass of tea and a sugar cube by her side, and gave Mashie her tea with milk—the tea bag still inside—and a half slice of marble cake.

Already bored with the card game, Laura sat on the swinging couch and began doodling in the pad, her brown pigtails swaying with her movements. Suddenly, she stopped pushing her feet off the ground and called me over.

"Look Mandy, what I found," she whispered, pointing to a sheet near the end of the pad.

All I could see was a yellowed page with rows of scores. "What is it?"

"Look again. Look at the names," she said.

There were three columns of numbers. The one with the winning score was headed Bill, my father, a close second was Laura's dad, Sol, and the third was entitled Benny. I gasped. A few times in the past, Laura and I heard our parents whisper about a man named Benny; but if we asked about him, the adults screwed up their faces and shooed us away. Now, we had his name on paper. This was the most proof we ever had; and with a smirky nod from Laura, I decided it was time to act.

Grandma Sarah was gathering her cards. I tapped her shoulder.

"What?" she asked. "You know I need to concentrate."

"Laura and I found something in this old pad."

"What's to find? Who won in 1932?"

"No, look at the names." I pushed the page in front of her. "See this name, Benny. Can you tell us who he was now?"

All three grandmas dropped their cards on the table. No one spoke for a minute or so. Finally, Grandma Sarah said, "Just put the pad away and let us play in peace."

"Sarah," Mashie said, "maybe it's time to tell them already." With three husbands to her name, Mashie was a woman who knew what it was like to be whispered about.

The grandmas started arguing in Yiddish, which they did whenever they didn't want us to know what they were saying. After years of trying to make out their conversations, I understood enough to realize that my tiny, white-haired Grandma Sarah had the last word and that the subject was closed.

•   •   •

The women picked up their cards. Mrs. Coffee made a joke about getting nothing but *dreck*, and the game started for real. Maybe this Benny person was even worse than I had thought. Tomorrow, Laura and I would come up with a better plan to get information. Laura resumed swinging on the couch, leafing through a Mickey Mouse comic book. I circled the women, trying to peek over their shoulders at their cards.

"Hey *vants*, stop moving all over," Mashie said to me.

"What's a *vants*?"

"A little bedbug. Someone who's creeping around." As Mashie spoke, she hummed and raised her eyebrows, giving me a signal that she had something good.

As I tiptoed toward Mashie's hand, I noticed Sarah and Rose putting their cards in place. Just as each grandma had her own style of baking, each held her cards in a different way. My grandma Sarah spaced her cards neatly but widely, fanning them out over the fingers of her small liver-spotted hand. Mashie held her cards every which way, some popping up, some clumped together. They never fell out, but they always looked like they were about to. She used both hands and often sifted the cards from hand to hand.

But it was Mrs. Coffee's hand that was the funniest. Her cards were so close—showing just enough corner so she could make out the number or letter—that it looked like she had one-third as many as Mashie's; and she fit them all in her right palm, pressed tightly on the right inside by her thumb, and on the left by her pinky. Players who didn't know Mrs. Coffee grew nervous when they saw three fingers from the outside, figuring she might be cheating and giving someone a sign.

"Mrs. Coffee," I said. "I see your pinky is up again."

Mrs. Coffee laughed and tried to put her pinky back over the cards, but it had a mind of its own and, before long, popped straight up in front.

"Gin!" Grandma Sarah screamed.

"A *shanda*!" Mashie said. "A shame. A real shame. I only needed one."

"*Gonif*, she's a *gonif*," Mrs. Coffee said.

"What's a *gonif?* I asked."

"A thief."

"But she didn't steal anything."

"Don't be fooled by your sweet little grandmother," Mrs. Coffee said. "She invites us over and robs us blind."

The women laughed, and I gathered my grandma Sarah's pennies that she collected from the kitty and arranged them in neat piles.

"Laura, come inside," my aunt Virginia called. "You too, Mandy."

"We'll be right in. Just fifteen more minutes!" I said.

•   •   •

"I need to stretch my legs," Mashie said, and the women decided to take a five-minute break. Sarah and Rose went in the house to use the toilet; Laura announced that she was going to the kitchen for a snack. I sat with Mashie on the Sun House steps while she lit a Parliament, but it was me who inhaled.

"So, Gram," I said, "I want to ask you a question."

"*Nu?*"

"Are you going to tell me who was Benny? I know he was or is someone special."

"*Oy-oy-oy!* I knew this was coming."

"And?"

"Darling, I wish I could tell you. But it is not up to me. It is not my secret to tell."

"So, it is a secret? But whose is it?"

"If I told you, it wouldn't be such a secret."

Mashie squeezed my cheek and said, "Some lucky man is going to get you. I should only live to go to your wedding."

"Why would I get married if it would end your life?"

"Don't be such a Smart Aleck," she said and gave me a wink.

I heard the kitchen door slam, and Grandma Sarah headed for us. I lost my chance to find out anything from Mashie, but if anyone would weaken, it would be her.

"What are you two whispering about?" Grandma Sarah asked as she bypassed us to open the Sun House door.

"Nothing," I said, following her. I scrambled to her side. I didn't want her to think I liked Mashie better.

Mashie sat in her chair and lit up another cigarette. Sarah cleared her throat and followed with a barrage in Yiddish. I not only listened intently but studied her lips, which sometimes helped me with the meanings. I understood the words "*mayn* Benny" and "*tsuris*" or troubles. Then my "sweet little" Grandma Sarah stood as tall as her almost five feet and jabbed her finger into Mashie's temple and said, loudly, *"Farshtais?"* or "Do you understand?"

Mashie's long nose flared like a dragon and I recognized that killer look. I tugged at her sleeve.

Mrs. Coffee entered and took her seat. "*Nu,*" she said. "Are we playing or what?"

Mashie started to deal, and Mrs. Coffee placed each card carefully in her three fingers. "Umm," Mrs. Coffee said. I stood on her right side and tried to peer into her hand, but she held it too close to her drooping breasts.

"Oh, Mrs. Coffee, have a sweet roll," I said. As she reached out her left hand across her chest, I managed to see her cards. Two nines; a one, two, three of clubs; two queens; and a mishmash of other cards. Then I looked at the money. My grandma Sarah was winning; Mrs. Coffee was even; Mashie had six pennies left. I slunk over to Mashie. It was easy to see her cards.

Mrs. Coffee threw out a six. My grandma Sarah picked it up and threw a jack. Mashie took a card from the deck and was about to throw a nine. I poked her back. She nodded and threw out a ten. After a few minutes, Mashie screamed, "Gin!"

Like I said, I always rooted for the loser.

THE CANDY STORE

It was 9:30 on an August Saturday morning, yet the air was as hot and steamy as the dishwashing alcove in the windowless Shady Grove Hotel kitchen. I hated to rest during daylight, especially in the morning, but I felt like I'd just eaten a giant matzo ball. I was so weak that, in my damp bathing suit, I slumped on the green Adirondack chair in front of our country house, pinned up my ponytail with two large bobby pins, and collapsed into a feverish state.

"Anyone ready for the first shift? I'm leaving in ten minutes sharp," my father called, standing on the lawn.

My cousin Laura lay on a damp towel by the apple trees, her pigtails spread like wet paintbrush tips. Grandma Sarah sat on the steps outside the kitchen, a glass of iced tea perched on her crossed knees. Nothing and nobody stirred. We were hoping for a sudden storm.

My father cleared his throat and wiped his thick lips with the back of his hand. "Well," he said, his gruff voice little more than a whisper. "I'm not going later. This is the final warning."

My mother's slanted shadow pressed the kitchen screen door, which gave way. She abruptly appeared. The morning was never a good time for her, and there was no telling her mood when she had to move in hundred-degree weather. She spoke in a thick Chesterfield exhale: "Mandy, Laura, you girls will come with us. Laura's family and Grandma will leave later. Brenda! Where is your sister? Brenda, get out here! We don't have all day."

Saturday was Village Day. Long-staying hotel guests and bungalow-colony renters went to town on Saturday. It was the only day the men, who worked in the city during the week, were there with their cars and all the stores were open. Mountainview had a movie theater, a clothing shop, a shoe store, and plenty of places to buy gum and comics, but the town was no fun when it was too hot. Drivers fought over the parking spaces closest to the stores; shoppers grumbled and shopkeepers were mean. My father wouldn't park in the sun because the steering wheel and dark seats would be burning when we got back. Then he'd curse all over or send me for ice cubes from the nearest store to smear on the sweaty leather before he'd sit. My mother would scream that she had to stand on a long line in the butcher shop, suffocating from the smell of sawdust floors and bloodied chops.

No, a Saturday trip to town was no picnic when it was hot. That's why we tried to get there as early as possible.

Brenda, Laura, and I climbed in the already boiling back seat.

"Ouch, I burned my tush!" Brenda cried. She took out a compact from her purse and balanced it on her knees. Focusing on a whitish pimple on her chin, she positioned her fingers for a good squeeze. Used to a smooth, rosy complexion that went with her black/brown shoulder-length hair, Brenda was a maniac about pimples, inspecting every bump several times a day.

Before we leaned back, Laura picked up a rag from the floor and laid it across the back seat. My parents got in the car, and my father backed out of the driveway. Two of the six Ratner dogs barked from our neighbor's yard.

"Even the dogs are too hot to bark," my mother said.

"It's a scorcher all right. The radio said it would be a record," my father said.

That was one of the few times my parents agreed on anything.

"Are they making a song about today's weather?" Laura asked.

"Why do you ask?"

"You said the heat would be a record."

Everyone laughed. I explained to Laura what my father meant. Usually, something like that would embarrass her, but it was even too hot for that, and she shrugged. Being a year older, months from being ten, I constantly worried that she'd feel hurt.

Before long, my father said, "Girls, you'd better get ready. We're about to pass Woodville."

"Oh no, not again," Brenda said, shaking her head. "It's been three years since that boy died."

Laura and I looked at each other, bent our heads into our laps, held our breaths, and pinched our noses until my father yelled "safe." Then we let out a swoosh of held-back breath. Once again, we had escaped polio.

"You girls are so infantile. Ohh, infantile, get it, infantile paralysis."

"What's that, Brenda?" Laura asked. She idolized Brenda and didn't recognize that my sister rarely had anything nice to say.

"Ask your buddy there. She already has it. A paralyzed brain."

"No more than yours," I said.

"You girls won't have to duck much longer," my mother said. "They're giving the polio vaccination at school this fall."

I thought of a boy in my class who wore leg braces, a girl in Brenda's school who died, and President Roosevelt in his wheelchair, and I was terrified that it was just a matter of time before I had to live in something called an iron lung. Never in my life had I been so happy to know I'd be getting a shot.

We passed the multistory laundry, and my mother said, "At least we don't have to work there on a day like today."

"Can you imagine, in this weather?" Brenda asked.

"Well, *I* certainly can," my mother said. "I used to work there all summer, in all kinds of conditions, pressing and folding all the hotels' linens."

Laura and I stared at my mother, whose head flicked back and forth as she addressed us in the back seat. It was times like these that I was convinced she had superhuman powers.

After the laundry, River Road ended, and we drove up a little slope onto Pleasant Road, a wide street leading into Mountainview. Even though Pleasant Road wasn't the main street, I liked it the most because it had the town's best stores, including a drugstore with a makeup counter and pinball machines, and a luncheonette with juicy hamburgers and tiny table jukeboxes.

A few buildings down was my favorite place in town, Isidore's Candy/Toy Store, where my father was lucky to find a parking spot. Usually, Brenda and I went shopping with my mother and helped her carry the bags, or my father picked us up. Occasionally, she sent my father to the hardware store or the lumberyard. Today, though, my mother said it was too hot to cook or fix anything. She was buying a few items and would go herself. "You girls can wait in Isidore's with your father," she said

Isidore and his wife, Olga, were my great-uncle and great-aunt. My grandma Sarah was Olga's older sister. Both short, thin, and pale, Isidore and Olga lived in a tiny, dark four-room apartment in the back of the store. Unlike us and the resort people at the hotels and bungalow colonies, they were townies and lived in Mountainview year-round. They had a married daughter, a Miami teacher, and a son, a pharmacist who ran a drugstore in a "godforsaken" state somewhere west of Chicago.

A rope ran across one of Isidore's store windows. It held a line of rubber swimming tubes: big, black smoothed-out inner tubes; yellow-and-orange waist roosters with long necks and beaks that squeaked; thin white donuts with Mickey Mouse characters; and red-plaid, ridged rafts. Attached to the rope by metal clasps were green snorkels, rust-colored rubber eye masks, swimming caps, frog flippers, beige nose clips, ear plugs, bottles of suntan oil, visors, sunglasses, reflectors—so much stuff for the sun and pool that I wondered if anyone could just take a plain swim.

I squeezed the rooster's beak, and the squeak must have let my uncle Isidore know that there were customers milling outside because he came out of the store and shook my father's hand. Normally, he didn't move from behind the cash register—even when my mother visited.

We went inside the dark store and, hearing our voices, my aunt Olga opened their apartment door at the far end. Except for weak rays filtered from the crowded display windows, the light in Isidore's came from two bare bulbs—one over the soda fountain and one over the toy area.

While my father sat on a fountain stool, sipping a glass of seltzer and talking baseball with Isidore, Brenda moved near the window to a tall rack of magazines and comic books. Laura and I dashed over to the toy section to see what was new. We surveyed the shelves in the two aisles, noting the dolls, balls, stuffed animals, and puzzle books. We ran our fingers along the dusty edges of game boxes, and Laura moved to the section set aside for arts and crafts.

"Daddy, I'm going to the drugstore," Brenda announced, pushing open the front door.

"Don't take all morning," my father said. "I don't want to go looking for you."

"Girls, here," we heard a faint voice from across the toy aisle. Aunt Olga held a finger vertically over her lips and waved us over. When we got to her, I felt dizzy from the lack of air and the musty odor. Olga's sparse, dyed-black hair edged her forehead with perspiration, and I smelled her rosewater talcum powder. She lifted a wet-stained, closed carton from the corner, opened the flaps, stuck her hand inside, and pulled out a bunch of chocolate bars. "Here take, take," she whispered. "But don't tell Uncle Isidore. Stick them in your pockets."

"But he'll see the bulges! He'll think we stole them," I said.

We each took two candy bars so my aunt wouldn't feel bad, but I was very nervous and walked funny with my arms stiffly over my hips so nobody could see my side pockets. My father patted the black-leather swivel stool next to him and said, "Sit down, girls. Izzy, how about two egg creams for them?"

I hopped on the stool, shocked at how nice my father was acting. I hadn't had a good egg cream in ages. Uncle Isidore poured a little milk and spritzed chocolate syrup into one of the paper soda cups that fit like a funnel into a steel holder. He sprayed seltzer, stirred it with a long spoon, and handed the drink to Laura. Then Isidore said to me, "Vanilla, right?" Without waiting for an answer, he pressed the vanilla dispenser.

The drink was cool and delicious, and I slurped it breathlessly through a candy-striped paper straw. I chewed the tip of my straw, and the drink got clogged, so I had to finish the rest by gulping from the cup. When Laura got to the end of her drink, she honked and wheezed air into her straw. Her eyes enlarged with delight when Isidore poured her a little more milk, which she mixed with the syrup left in the bottom of her cup.

Two boys came in the store and lingered in front of the candy display, elbowing each other. They picked up and examined colored little boxes and wrapped paper twists, and then put them back.

"Boys don't touch the merchandise," Isidore said. "People have to eat that. What do you want anyway?"

"We'll have a Baby Ruth and four of them baseball-card gum packets."

"That will be twenty-five cents. Do you have the money?"

The boys took out change from their pockets and counted. They had twenty-two cents.

"Sorry, boys. Come back when you have three more pennies."

"Come on, Izzy. Don't be such a cheapskate," my father said.

"Oh, Mr. Sweater Millionaire. No wonder you're having business problems. How would I make a living if I let everyone get away without paying?"

My father reached into his pants pocket and threw three pennies on the counter. The boys gathered the candy and gum, and mumbled, "Hey, thanks a lot, mister. Yeah, thanks a lot."

I glanced at my father and smiled. He looked handsome, leaning over to sip his drink. I gazed up at the big round clock on the wall and remembered how he had taught me to tell time when I was in the first grade. Every day after dinner, I'd sit on his lap while he showed me with his hands how twelve o'clock was like a praying position, nine o'clock was two palms at a right angle, and six o'clock was one hand straight up and the other straight down.

"You're a sucker, Bill," my uncle said as the boys slammed the door.

"And Isidore, you're an old Jew."

There was silence, and I fidgeted in my stool, re-clasping my hair clip. I was pretty sure my father was kidding with Isidore. He might have said a bad word about a Negro or someone Spanish, but I didn't think he'd mean it about a Jew. I once heard my father tell Brenda about the two years he thought he was going to be a doctor. He had to go to medical school in Canada because of something called a quota of Jews. That meant that the schools in America accepted a certain number of Jewish people and couldn't have more. Since that time, my father said he knew how it felt to be a Jew. But when Isidore laughed, I knew it was okay.

"Maybe I'm an old Jew, but at least I act like one," Isidore said. "You and your brother could be Catholics for all I can tell. You have a Christmas tree in your own home. I bet you haven't stepped foot in a synagogue since your own bar mitzvah."

"I stepped inside."

"Yeah, probably to use the toilet."

My father grumbled, stood, and said he was going to put water in the car. Isidore reached over the counter to take away our empty drink cups, wiggling his finger at us the same way Aunt Olga did. We strained our necks over the counter. "Shh, here take these. But don't tell your father and please don't tell Olga." Uncle Isidore opened his fist over mine and then over Laura's. I felt something small and cold and stuffed it inside my pocket, next to the candy bars. When we got outside, I fished in my pocket and took it out. It was a dime! It was too bad I had to keep it secret because the best place to spend it was in Isidore's store.

Laura went to the drugstore to get Brenda. My mother appeared in the distance, carrying three bags of groceries. My father and I were alone on the sidewalk. I pulled his shirt a few times to divert his attention from lighting his cigar.

"What?" he asked, mopping his forehead with a handkerchief.

"I heard Uncle Isidore say something about your business. Is something wrong at the factory?"

"Do you have to know everything?" he shouted.

"I was just asking."

"Well, you don't have to know."

"Maybe I could help."

"Help, schmelp. What could you do? You're just a stupid kid."

Tears clouded my vision, and I rubbed them away with my shirtsleeves. My father opened the trunk, clearing his throat and spitting on the ground. His face grew uglier before my eyes. His cheeks were a sooty color and drooped like the stuffed squirrel whose acorn-pouched face smacked against Isidore's window display. I couldn't look at him anymore and turned to see my mother approaching us on Main Street, the long avenue that cut through the railroad tracks.

Brenda and Laura joined us, and we helped my mother put the groceries in the trunk.

"It was just murder in that butcher shop," my mother said, combing her fingers through her damp-edged brown hair. A smear of ruby lipstick stained her front teeth.

"It was no picnic here," my father said.

"What did you have to do besides listening to Isidore and Olga?" my mother asked in a tired and snippy voice.

We piled into the car. The brown leather seats were scorching, and I squatted onto the rubber floor mat, a cooler alternative.

"Nothing, what do I ever have to do?" my father said, rolling down his window. "You're the one with the big plans. How much did you spend anyway?"

"What does it matter?"

"You probably bought a coupla lobsters just to spite me. Yeah, girls, your mother only knows to buy a coupla this and a coupla that. You never know when we will be starving."

I could feel my heartbeat quicken. My mother's extended family died in Poland during the war. I didn't know all the stories, but I had heard often enough that they had no food. "Daddy didn't mean anything, Mommy," I said. My mother turned and smiled. I couldn't think of another word to say to stop them from being nasty to each other.

"The rag is dirty," Laura said, fingering it up in a tweezer motion from the seat. "Why don't we spread our coloring books and sit on them." Her voice was loud and forced. Even though Laura was more of a scaredy-cat than I was, she had a lot of experience changing subjects with her parents.

My mother dug into her red leather pocketbook. "Here's your lousy change." She smacked three dollar bills on my father's lap.

"That's all?" my father exploded. "What did you buy, four sirloins? Only the best for your mother, girls."

"Don't involve the girls in your sarcasm, Bill."

I looked into the butcher bag that was on the floor near my feet. I noticed a big orange-brown wrapped package. With my pinky, I flipped open a fold and saw bits of chopped meat stuck to the paper. I had been with my mother many times at the butcher shop. Surely, she would have insisted, "Lean, Lenny. Make sure it's extra lean." I flicked open the wrapping, and the meat looked ropey and not as red as usual. It smelled like the bag of sprouting squishy potatoes I discovered in the pantry that had been left from last summer. I poked around the bag and found a longer, thinner package that felt lumpy and squiggly. I flipped open a crease, and a scrawny, wrinkled chicken foot popped out. "I yelled, "Ugh." My grandma Sarah would use this for chicken soup.

Laura peeked inside. "Ohh, that's disgusting."

Brenda said, "Close that package. The smell is nauseating."

"What are you doing with that meat, Mandy?" my mother asked.

"Nothing," I said. "But Daddy, Mommy bought hamburger meat, not steak."

"Sure," he said, "you'd defend your mother if she bought a Cadillac." He turned the key in the ignition, and the engine started to putter and then rev.

"Wait, Bill," Isidore yelled, running after our car and waving papers in his hand. "Here, I forgot that I got mail yesterday for you from the post office."

Miracle of miracles, in the packet was a letter for me, from Francine. I had written three letters to her, and she hadn't answered. I thought she had forgotten me. This letter was postmarked July 6th, and nobody could understand how it could take a month to travel from Brooklyn to Mountainview, except my mother said things hadn't changed that much since she had been a teenager waiting for mail from a boy she liked who had moved to the Bronx.

I ripped open the letter and hugged it close to me as I read it to myself in the back seat, leaning against the car window. It said:

> *Dear Mandy,*
>
> *Hi, how are you? I can't wait to come visit you in August. I can't wait to see all the places you always talk about and to have a real adventure with you and your cousin Laura. Brooklyn is so bor-ing without you here. I go to Brighton Beach as much as I can. A few times I played ball with Marie-Anne and the other Catholic girls on our block. Once we went swimming together in Rockaway. It was okay. I miss you.*
>
> *Love and kisses, Francine.*

I sat still for a while, thinking of Francine's puppy-dog nose and freckled cheeks. I poked my head out the window, trying to feel a breeze. In my mind, I started writing a letter back to her, saying, me too, Francine, I can't wait for you to come. What I wouldn't write was to coax her away from Marie-Anne who was always trying to take Francine away from me.

Meanwhile, Brenda was admiring her new nail-care kit that she had bought in the drugstore. Inspecting Laura's chewed-up stubs, Brenda promised my cousin that she could give her a manicure that would bring new life to her nails. Wanting to get Laura's attention, I pulled one of her pigtails closer to me.

"What, Mandy? Can't you see Brenda is showing me something?"

"Yeah, I can see. I just . . . never mind." Let Brenda snip off Laura's fingers for all I cared. Laura was always a sucker for my sister's girly things. I was tempted to not even warn Laura when we were about to pass Woodville. But I couldn't, not when it came to my cousin getting polio.

"Laura!"

"What Mandy, I told you I'm busy."

"I know, but you have to duck. Hurry!"

"Look what you did!" Brenda screamed. You made me drop the nail file and scissors. Mandy, you'd better not come back up without them."

"Me? What did *I* do?" I said, hunched with my cousin, pressing my mouth to Laura's ear.

"Oh, what did your friend Francine write?" Laura asked as we retrieved my sister's nail supplies. "Can I read it?"

"She's looking forward to visiting us soon. I'll show you at the house."

When it was safe, we crawled back on the seat.

"Here," I said, stretching my arm to Brenda. "Here are your precious nail instruments. Now you'll be able to scratch Bruce Reiger's back."

"Mother! Will you tell your bratty daughter to shut her mouth?"

"Why don't we all shut up," my mother said.

"All of you, please I can't hear myself think," my father shouted.

Laura looked at me and mouthed the words, "B-R-U-C-E R-E-I-G-E-R." That set me off, and I couldn't hold back the giggles, which set Laura off. Now my laughing was coming quicker and louder, and my whole body was heaving.

My mother turned and scrunched her eyebrows, took in a breath, and exhaled in an explosion, "Amanda Gerber!" Her lips were tightly pursed, causing tiny vertical lines around her mustache area. At that moment, she looked like a monkey, and that thought got me going even worse. The sounds that came out of my mouth were a combination of hiccupping and gasping, and my chest ached from stabbing pain. Without warning, sobs pushed out, and my face was a mess of snot and tears.

Suddenly, the brakes squeaked, and the car lurched. I fell forward, my forehead banging on the back of the driver's seat. The car stopped in the middle of the road. Slowly, my father put the car in reverse and backed up until we were at Woodville. Then he hit the brake again, and we stopped in Woodville's parking lot.

"Bill, what happened?" my mother screamed.

"What happened, what happened? I'll tell you what happened. You raised a bunch of hysterical hyenas who don't know how to keep their traps shut. I can't take it anymore. Mandy, get out of the car."

"What are you saying, Bill?" my mother asked.

"Mandy is old enough to go home by herself. Maybe after twenty minutes of walking, she'll learn to control herself."

"But Uncle Bill, what about the polio? Mandy can't get out here."

"She can and she will." He got out of the car and opened the door that I was leaning against. I slipped out and fell to the ground. My father grabbed the back of my blouse and yanked me up. I was trembling but managed to brush dirt from my shorts and move my legs until I could take a few steps.

"Get back in the car, Mandy," my mother yelled. "It's too hot to be walking."

"I won't ride in this car again," I said, my voice cracking.

Within seconds, my father was behind the wheel again and started the car, inching up the road. Before he had a chance to stop and order me back, I ran ahead of the car, in the same direction but moving to the passenger side so my father couldn't reach me. There was a car's slamming sound, followed by screeching and a revving. I didn't swivel to look and felt the rush of hot air as my father's car sped ahead of me. I heard the fading of my mother's screams.

I felt the pounding and crunching of nearby footsteps on the tar and gravel road. Fingers drilled into my back, and I turned, terrified it was a monster that was hiding in the bushes, or worse, my father who had somehow gotten out of the car and lurked behind me.

"Laura, it's you!"

"Oh, Mandy."

"Hurry. Try to catch up with the car. It's dangerous, the polio."

"Oh, it doesn't matter, Mandy. If you get it, I'll get it. Besides, I think we're far enough away from Woodville anyhow."

The bottom of Laura's orange strap-tied halter top left tight lines against her pudgy stomach, and her sweaty cheeks were stained with soot. Wanting to hug her, I knew that she got embarrassed by affection, so I squeezed her sticky hand.

"Thanks, Laura, for getting out."

"We're blood cousins, aren't we?" she said.

"Yes, we are." A few times in the past month, I wasn't so sure Laura had taken our vows seriously. Once I even suspected she had been sorry she allowed me to prick her finger with a sharpened bobby pin. But now I was sure. No matter how crazy my family was, Laura was behind me even if it meant being paralyzed for life.

FLOATING IN THE NEVERSINK

On a Saturday morning in late August, a rusty-black 1940 Cadillac Town Car drove up the driveway of our country house in the Catskills. Though I loved that car with its silver flying goddess pointing the way ahead and its silver-edged running board that we could step onto, I also hated what it stood for. Across the side in big gold capital letters were the words, Futterman's Funeral Home, and underneath was the address in Sheepshead Bay, Brooklyn. Mr. Futterman stood in the open-topped front section, his black fedora dusty from the long ride, and his wife, Lois, clung alongside and waved her black patent-leather pocketbook, shouting, "We're here" as if we wouldn't notice a big fifteen-year-old funeral car taking up our entire driveway. My aunt Virginia, normally dressed in a hot-pink halter and shorts, wore a black straight skirt and white blouse, the proper attire to welcome her older sister's family whose sometimes Orthodox views wouldn't allow them to drive on Saturday—except when they wouldn't see anyone they knew like here on River Road in Mountainview.

I didn't pay much attention to Lois Futterman unloading shopping bags of food, including bagels and herring in cream sauce, figuring I would be tasting these delicacies as soon as we sat to eat in the house. I was focused on my cousin Laura, who, like her mother seemed to have changed into another person. Instead of her usual shirt with the gray poodle on the pocket, she wore dark-blue pedal pushers and a starched sleeveless white blouse, and her usual pigtailed copper-brown hair was parted on the side and held in place with an oval tortoiseshell barrette. Despite her attire, my cousin jumped up and down until her cousins, twelve-year-old Janie and eight-year-old Marty, Laura's age and a year younger than me, were wrapped in her arms.

Last month on our secret rock, Laura and I had become blood cousins and, a few days ago, she confessed that I was her very best cousin. It was hard to believe all that sworn loyalty from the way she was hanging over her cousins. Okay, they were related through their mothers, and Laura and my fathers were brothers, but Laura never mentioned any special fondness for them. She even complained that Marty picked his nose a lot. Laura once caught him putting his finger in his mouth afterward.

Laura's cousins brought her a paint-by-numbers set; one of those wood paddles with a reddish-brown ball hanging from a gray-rubber string stapled to the middle of the wood; and a Slinky, which Laura immediately took out of the cardboard box and curved down the Sun House steps.

The cousins gathered around Laura, examining the toys and taking turns with the paddle. They weren't too good; the rubber string tangled when they swung the paddle hard, and they missed the ball completely. I stood on the side of the Sun House, dying to show Laura's cousins my trick—to wrap the string twice around the handle so that it was shorter and easier for the ball to reach the round part of the paddle. The last time I tried that in Uncle Isidore's toy store in the village, I got up to forty-six hits before my uncle told me to put it back on the shelf. I never got a turn with Laura's because her cousins grabbed it from each other.

Soon, Aunt Virginia opened the kitchen door and told Laura to bring her cousins in the house to eat breakfast. "Come, kids," Laura said, looking at Janie who was trying to straighten the Slinky. "Leave the toys. Mandy will put them away for us." Then, turning to me, she said, "You'll leave them on top of the trunk in the Sun House for us, won't you, Mandy?"

"Sure," I said, then waited for Laura to add something about me coming inside. I thought again about what my aunt had said, and I was almost sure it was "bring your cousins." Laura must have forgotten I was her cousin, too. I felt like I was going to cry but swallowed it in a lump. Besides, I told myself, Francine was coming to visit me soon. I would show Laura what true loyalty was.

Finally, I got my feet to move and took the toys into the Sun House. I sat on the stained, green-fern glider couch and rocked back and forth, every few minutes stopping the motion with my foot on the floor, thinking that maybe someone had called me; but the squeak of the couch was harsh, and I couldn't hear anything but faraway sounds from Ratner's peeling, dirty-white bungalows. For a long while, I sat and rocked and stopped and listened until my mother tapped on the gazebo's screen window.

"Mandy, are you deaf?"

"What?" I asked, about to jump out of my skin.

"I called you several times."

"Why? Did someone want me to go inside?"

"No, I just wanted to tell you where I'm going. I can't take it inside that house a minute longer. The Futtermans are driving me crazy with their packages of food and what to eat with what, and how much everything cost."

"But you can't go anywhere. How about Francine?"

"Do you realize what time it is?"

"What?"

"It's only ten in the morning. Francine's not coming until noon. She's going to stop first at the hotel where her grandmother is staying. I'll be at Siegel's for a while. I need to pick up some laundry powder and milk from the concession. I'll be back in plenty of time."

"Are you sure Mrs. Nederlander said noon?"

"I'm sure. Do you want to come? You can visit with Barbara Siegel."

I thought of the small concession shop at Siegel's. Located in the entrance of the clubhouse, the concession sold groceries and household supplies and served coffee and sandwiches. Mr. and Mrs. Siegel's granddaughter Barbara often hung out there because she said the boy who worked behind the counter looked like Sal Mineo, her idol but to me a bummy greaser.

"No. I'll wait here. I want to see Francine drive up."

I leaned back on the couch, closed my eyes, and continued to rock, imagining Laura's cousins leaving, and Laura joining me and Francine. We could search the little brown pads in the Sun House trunk to see if we could find out more about the mysterious man in our family named Benny. Maybe my best friend and my best cousin (or my former best cousin), and I could find more clues. All I knew for sure was that there was a score in the pad with his name on it and a date of 1932, twenty-three years ago. Relatives had mentioned his name a few times over the years, but then everyone in earshot immediately changed the subject. Clearly, this Benny character did something awful. My thoughts were going crazy, picturing possible explanations. What if we found out that Benny was a murderer and we had to turn him in to the Mountainview police? Or what if he was Uncle Isidore's lost son and had married a Catholic woman and run away to Monticello?

•   •   •

Long minutes passed, and I decided to head down the driveway and look for Francine's car. That way, I'd make sure she didn't miss the house. I searched for a place to sit at the end of the driveway to get a good view of both directions. Most people came from the village side, but I wasn't sure where Francine's grandmother was staying so I had to scan the riverside just in case. The best spot was on the grassy area in front of our house, just before the road started. After every other car passed, I glanced up the driveway to see if Laura was standing there, in case she was ready to apologize for ignoring me.

I sat on the grass with my knees folded out Indian style, jerking my head from side to side to check in both directions and pulling blades of grass with my fingers like I was plucking the strings of a harp. Worried that I was causing bald spots, I grabbed a big black-eyed Susan in my hand and eased out the slim gold petals, one by one, singing to myself, "He loves me, he loves me not." I prayed that it came out "he loves me," even though I had no idea who the "he" was. I was in luck—"he loves me."

A blue car whizzed by. It looked like Francine's, but it didn't stop. Maybe her parents had the wrong directions. I jumped up and rushed down the road, toward the Neversink River, turning back every few seconds to see if a car was coming. I ran like a crazy person back to my house and scanned my driveway. Nothing new. I returned to the spot in front of my house. Could it be that she wasn't coming?

After the eighth blue car went by, I bent to pick a dandelion. I brought it to my mouth and puffed hard on the see-through, cotton-ball head as if I were trying to blow out all the candles on a birthday cake with one breath. White feathery fluffs exploded in the air, some settling on my wet lips. A few clumps clung to the weed's little-round top, like the balding head of an old lady. I heard a car beep and lifted my head. There was a brand-new 1955 blue Chevy coming toward me with an elbow jutting out the driver's window, its arm straight up, fingers pinching a cigarette to ash in the wind.

Then a skinny, suntanned arm flapped vigorously out the backseat window. As the car drove closer, a curly brown head popped out. I shook my hands high over my head, screaming, "Here! Here! Here!" Then, like the traffic guard at school, I motioned to Mr. Nederlander, easing his car up our driveway, latching onto Francine's arm as she hung out the side.

Francine and I hugged each other, leaping up and down, whooping like we just won a refrigerator on a quiz show. The Nederlanders stayed long enough to say hello to my family and excused themselves to return to Francine's grandmother's hotel. I had Francine for the whole day.

"Let me show you the house first, and then the pool at Siegel's, then Ratner's rocks, the Shady Grove Hotel, and maybe the river where we go swimming and fishing all the time," I said. Then, almost out of breath, I added, "Oh, there's a new little lake by the hotel, and we can go rowing."

"It all sounds good to me," Francine said.

I dragged Francine through the kitchen door where Laura's family was sitting at the table, strewn with packets of lox, carp, and white fish, still lying open in wax paper. The adults were drinking coffee, dipping prune danishes, and the children were playing Chutes and Ladders on the floor. I introduced Francine, and when Laura said nothing about us joining them, I led Francine in a quick sweep around the house. Afterwards, we went into the Sun House, and I showed her the window ledges, wooden rows of carved-out spaces filled with small toys and art supplies.

"Can I try that?" she asked, pointing to Laura's new wood paddle, lying on the trunk.

"Well, it's Laura's . . . but I guess she wouldn't mind."

Francine pounded away at the ball but couldn't get past three. Then, she swatted upward so hard that the rubber string slipped off the staple and the ball flew up, hit the screen door, bounced off the walls, and rolled under the couch.

"Oh, no, I broke it!"

"Don't worry. Maybe we can fix it."

We squatted and tried to squeeze our arms under the couch to reach the ball. I slid my back under, finally got my hands around the ball, and then dragged myself out, my shorts trailing dust.

"Ahchoo!"

"Bless you, Francine. Do you have a cold?"

"It's my hay fever. It gets worse whenever I go near fields or flowers." The freckles on her nose seemed to dance.

"That's terrible." At once, I worried about all the green around. "We'd better fix this thing," I said, poking through the window ledges for a stapler. I found a small one and tried to staple the string back into the wood paddle. When I finally got a staple in, the string kept falling out. The only way it would stay was with black masking tape.

The kitchen door opened, and Laura and her cousins came into the Sun House. Janie, who was the oldest and bossiest, picked up the paddle, now lying on the chair, and drew her hand backward. "Hey what's this?" she asked, running her fingers along the shiny, black strip.

"Tape," I said.

Laura gave me a dirty look. "Mandy, did you use my new paddle?"

"Yes, I'm sorry Laura. I did."

"Without asking me!"

"Since when do I have to ask you? We always share our things."

"And you broke it!"

"I said I was sorry." Just when Francine was about to say something, I poked her and said to Laura, "Don't worry, I'll never touch your stuff again!

Come on Francine, let's go ask my mother if we can go ROWING." I wanted Laura to hear in the worst way since Aunt Virginia wouldn't let her precious daughter go anywhere near the lake without an adult. As it happened, my mother wouldn't either, but Laura didn't know that. I led Francine down the driveway in the direction of the new Shady Grove lake as if we were going there anyway.

As Francine and I got to the end of the driveway, Ratner's handyman Lester came out of his shack with two dogs tied to ropes. The dogs yelped and hissed. Francine ran to my other side, away from the road, and pulled my arms, whimpering.

"That's Lester," I said. "Should we go and talk to him?"

"Mandy, no. Hurry, let's run down the road. He looks like a killer I saw in the newspaper. And his dogs are like those wolves that eat children!"

"Calm down," I said, pretending nothing was wrong. But I was scared that the dogs would break away and snap when they saw a strange girl. "They're tied up."

We ran anyway toward the Shady Grove lake. As we slowed, Francine said, "Thanks for taking the blame for the broken paddle. I was going to tell Laura that it was me."

"I know. She would have been madder if she knew I let you use it."

"Ahchoo! I need another tissue." Francine wiped her nose with the back of her hand.

"Are you okay? Your eyes are puffing out and getting red."

"That happens with my hay fever."

Since we couldn't go rowing, I was still determined to have an adventure. Maybe it wouldn't be about Benny, but at least it would be something I could brag to Laura about. We skipped pebbles in the lake, crossed the road, trudged up Shady Grove's tar driveway, and walked into Ratner's, heading behind the garage that joined our two properties. Large boulders marked the end of Ratner's, extending along the width of our land. There were smaller rocks piled in front of a larger one, so it was easy to climb to the very top.

"Wow!" Francine said as she saw the huge rocks, which looked bigger and bigger as we got closer. "I don't think I can get up those."

"Come on, Francine, it isn't so bad. It just looks high from here. Once you're up this big one, the other rocks aren't so steep." I couldn't understand why Francine hesitated. On our block in the city, we often climbed the top of a high, slanted dumpster to reach the back alleys of stores where we played cops and robbers.

I stepped on a small rock and placed my foot in a wide crack. I lifted myself to the top of the big rock and helped pull up Francine. We stood on the flat part of the rock, facing the woods and inspected the scene.

"Let's go that way," I said, pointing toward Ratner's playground. "All we have to do is jump across this big rock onto that one, and there's a nice little waterfall. We can drink from it."

"We have to jump over that!" Francine stared into a deep canyon separating the two rocks. Her voice was a mix of almost-crying and almost-yelling.

"It's just like hopscotch. We've done that a million times by our dead end." I never realized before that Francine was such a chicken.

"But this is worse. We can fall down here."

"We won't. Believe me. Laura and I do it all the time, and she wears those special orthopedic shoes. Come, I'll help you."

I stood with my feet together, bent my knees, and gave a big jump onto the other rock.

"I don't know if I can do it." Francine peered into the dark drop, maybe fifteen feet below, and shook her head.

"Don't look down, just look at me."

Francine started to cry for real this time, and no matter how I encouraged her to jump, she wouldn't budge. "I can't," she sobbed. "I'm sorry, Mandy. I'm a big baby. I'm not as brave as you and Laura."

"Never mind. We can play on your rock, too." I jumped back and joined Francine on the flat part of her rock.

"Let's play Family," she said, cheering up as soon as we sat.

"Okay," I said. "What story should we do?"

"How about coming to the country?" Francine said, sniffling and swiping at her watery hay-fever eyes.

"Yeah, let's pretend that a man like Lester knocks on the door of our country house and asks to come inside."

"And then what?" A year younger than me at eight and a half, Francine, like Laura, counted on me to make up the plots.

"Maybe this man comes in to fix something," I said, "and when no one's looking, he steals a jar filled with dollar bills."

We didn't get any further with the story as we heard my mother yelling, "Mandy, Francine, where are you?"

Quickly, we climbed down and skipped the length of Ebbets Field toward our property. Francine and I held hands, swinging them, singing "I love to go a-wandering along the mountain track," from our favorite song, "The Happy Wanderer." As we got to the Sun House, we noticed my mother inside talking to Laura and her cousins.

"Oh, there you are," she said. "I've been looking for you. It's way past lunchtime. Aren't you girls hungry?"

"We're starving," I said, beckoning my mother to come out. I left Francine by the Sun House and told her to go inside and wait for me.

"What?" she asked me as I drew her to the apple trees, away from the Sun House.

"Did you ask Daddy if he'll drive us to the river? We can take sandwiches there and have a picnic and go swimming. Francine has her suit on underneath."

"Why don't you ask him yourself? He's in the front, napping in the hammock."

"But he'll be mad if I wake him."

"I think he's just dozing."

I charged down the hill to where a hammock was hooked to two oak trees on the right side of the front lawn. I cleared my throat a few times and made as much noise as I could with my feet, smushing the piles of leaves at the base of the trees.

"Do I hear a bird?" my father murmured.

"A bird with long brown hair."

"Oh, a harebrained bird."

"Come on, Daddy, you know it's me. Do you think, maybe if it's not too much trouble, you could drive us to the river?"

"Who's us? Are there other birdbrains around?"

"You know! Me and Francine."

"What happened to your sidekick, Laura?"

"We don't have to do everything together."

My father sat up a little and took out a stick match from his shirt pocket and flicked it on the tree bark. After four strikes, the match lit, and he breathed in deeply on his cigar until the tip glowed and settled into a good-sized ash.

"Well?"

He didn't answer but pointed to his moccasins under the hammock. After slipping them on, he lay back and clasped his hands under his head, like he was going to think and smoke some more.

I walked back up the hill and found my mother hiding behind the tallest pine tree near the Sun House.

"So?" she said.

"I don't know. He didn't say yes, and he didn't say no."

"That's a good sign. Why don't you go in the house, put on your bathing suit, take the sandwich bag out of the refrigerator, and get the blanket that's on the kitchen chair. When you come out, I'll bet your father is already in the car waiting."

Sure enough, by the time I got the stuff and picked up Francine, who was watching Laura and her cousins play Monopoly in the Sun House, my father was in the car, beeping his horn to his favorite rhythm, "shave and a haircut, shampoo."

We sat in the back seat, and I tried not to think of Laura and her cousins. Suddenly, my father beeped the horn four times.

"Why is he honking?" Francine asked.

"When we turn that bend, we have to beep because it's a blind turn: the other drivers can't see us coming, and we can't see them either." Just as we cleared the corner, I shouted, "See that stone bridge? It's the beginning of the river, the Neversink."

"Does that mean you never sink?" Francine asked.

"I'm not sure. Is that what it means, Daddy?"

"How the hell would I know? Don't ask me such dumb questions."

We drove farther down the road, and, between the trees along the river's edge, we caught glimpses of light sparkling on the brownish-green water like gold coins flipping from heads to tails. In a clearing, a man waded in the river, snapping his fishing pole above him like a conductor's baton, his line whipping and wiggling in the air, sinking out of sight.

"Quick, look to the left!" I said. "That's the Neversink Lodge, the nicest hotel around. See there's the golf course, the rowing lake, the pool. It's a real famous place. Sid Caesar comes here."

"Really?"

"Yeah, we saw him a few times."

We made a right onto a narrow rusted-green steel bridge, and my father honked again to warn oncoming drivers. Out the windows, the Neversink rolled in miniature white mountain peaks under us. We listened to clanks and rumbles, feeling the distant shake of the rickety wood slats as we moved like a tortoise to the other side. I looked behind me in the back seat and read the sign on top of the bridge: "Claussen's Bridge, Limit: 5 tons."

"Daddy, how much do we weigh?"

"Oh, you're about one ton, and Francine another ton."

"Oh, Mr. Gerber," Francine giggled. "Mandy, your father is always joking. He's so funny."

We parked the car in a grassy clearing, traipsing down a path leading to a large open area by the water's edge.

"Look Francine, a beach."

"That sandy place?" she asked.

"Yeah. Okay, it's not Brighton Beach, but you have to say it's cute."

"It's cute," she said.

We spread our blanket, sat, and opened the wax paper on our bologna sandwiches. As we ate, we watched a fisherman standing in knee-deep water to our right past the bridge, wearing high, shiny-black boots. On our left, two teenage boys swam, disappearing behind a boulder.

"What do you think those boys are doing?" I asked.

"Beats me," Francine said.

We stared at them until one boy threw something in the air, shouting, "Catch!" Then, we saw little puddles of suds circle from behind the rock, traveling along rows of currents toward the shore, clustering around the shallow water like foam on top of beer glasses.

"That's soap. They're taking a bath," my father said.

"In the river?" I asked.

"Why not, dummy? It's cleaner than your bathwater. Look down, it's so clear you can see millions of tadpoles and small fish."

"There are fish here?" Francine asked, raising her eyebrows.

"Of course, why do you think that man is fishing?" my father said.

"But, he's far away, closer to the other bridge. Are there fish here by the beach, where we'll go in the water?"

"Don't worry, Francine, they don't bite," I said, realizing she was scared here, too.

After we finished lunch, we took off our shirts and stretched on the blanket to sunbathe in our suits, lazily drawing designs in the wet sand with little sticks. Hundreds of tiny brown, gold, and white stones glistened in the sunlight by the shoreline. My father stood on a small rock in the shallow end, his pants rolled up to his knees. He followed the rocks in a zigzag pattern, going from one to the other, his legs growing wet until he stood on a rock in the middle of the river.

"Come in, girls! You've waited long enough after lunch."

"I don't know," Francine said.

I was getting disgusted with Francine's attitude. Laura would have been in the water already. For a second, I was ashamed of myself. For years,

Francine had stuck with me on our block even when the Catholics wanted to steal her away from me.

"What are you afraid of?" I asked, my voice softening. "I've seen you swim often enough at the Brighton Beach Baths' pool, and you go in the Atlantic."

"I know, it's just, I guess I don't like swimming in such a big place, with nothing to hold onto. I rarely go in the ocean, and when I do, I only wet my toes."

"Nothing's going to happen to you. Besides, my father is right there."

With me leading, we tiptoed from rock to rock until we were near my father.

"Now go in the water," my father said. "It's not deep."

I dunked in my toes and pushed my foot down to make sure I could feel the bottom. Then I jumped off the rock, and bubbly water instantly swirled around my waist. "It's not deep. Look Francine, I can stand. Come on in."

Francine joined me, and we stepped on the rocky bottom, stubbing our toes and springing when we thought we touched anything slimy or moving. Francine felt something sharp bite her foot and screamed. When she lifted her leg, she discovered that the awful, gobbling water creature wrapped around her toes was really a jumble of fishing line caught on a tin can.

"Whew," she said, and her voice seemed to calm.

My father leapt off his little rock into the water and waddled farther away near the boys, where the water was deeper, up to his neck.

"Daddy, you're not wearing a suit," I hollered. I could see his shirt and the belly of his pants swell.

"He looks like one of those crazy mirrors in Coney Island," Francine chuckled. "You know, the one that makes you fat and short and twisted?"

Though Francine stayed close to the rocks in the shallow water, I got brave and dog-paddled toward my father. I was afraid to swim out because I wasn't sure what was beneath me; but by dog-paddling, I could swat anything that got in my way.

I reached my father and swam around him.

"Why don't you float a little and give yourself a rest?" he asked.

"I can't really float."

"The way you swim, don't tell me your mother never taught you to float?"

"It's too scary."

"Come on, I'll hold you."

"Don't let go."

"I won't."

"Promise?"

"Okay, I promise."

My father held one hand under my waist, and with his other hand, tried to level my legs. "Stop moving all over. Just lie still."

I stretched out and leaned back. The river quivered under me like a thick blanket of Jell-O. I relaxed for a second or two before my father's hand dropped from under my waist, and something tugged at me. Afraid to upset myself, I stayed as flat as I could, but I drifted farther away. Soon I was carried by an unseen force. There was a big splash, my body somersaulted; and I felt like I was on a level escalator, rolling fast down the river, under Claussen's Bridge, away from the beach. I wheezed as the water filled my nose, and I struggled to keep my head above water. Thousands of little waves surrounded me, pulling me downstream, shoving me over rocks and against sharp tree stumps.

A jagged cliff came in my direction. I swung my arms, trying to shove away the menacing boulder when a snake-like object jutted from the rock's side like an extended frog's leg. My fingers grabbed the slimy creature, which turned out to be a thick branch, and I yanked with all my might, enough to avoid a direct hit to my chest, though my hips scraped the rock's sides as I dragged myself around the craggy stone. Just when I thought I was safe, a violent motion yanked my legs, and I continued to roll feet first, sucked along as if I were in a vacuum cleaner.

Finally, a big hand dragged me upstream toward the side, and hauled me onto the marshy shore, under the bridge. It was the fisherman.

"Are you okay, little girl?"

I was choking, coughing out water. I struggled to catch my breath.

"Mandy, Mandy!" my father garbled, approaching the shore. He gawked at my bloodied thighs, but when he saw that I was otherwise in one piece, he thanked the fisherman. I sat up and followed the river to the other side; Francine stood on the beach waving frantically at me. I waved back.

The fisherman returned to his spot, and my father and I sat in the grass for a few minutes trying to steady our heartbeats.

"You let go of me," I said.

My father didn't answer. He turned his back from me and curved his head down like he was examining his knees. His back was shaking, and his breathing was loud like when he was about to have one of his screaming nightmares, the ones my mother had said that I was too young to understand. I crossed my arms around myself. After what seemed like forever, he turned.

"You let go of me," I repeated, lowering my voice.

"Couldn't . . . you stay still?"

"But you let go of me." It seemed that was the only thing I could say.

"That's . . . how," he said, stopping to lick his lips, "that's how you learn to float."

"But you promised not to. And then you disappeared."

He gazed down the river, jerking his head in the opposite direction as if he were searching for someone. He repeated this gesture several times.

"Daddy?"

"I dropped my hand for a sec . . . ond, just a sec . . . ond," he stammered. His shoulders shuddered.

"You left me there," I sobbed.

"You pulled away . . . the current. Tried to catch up . . . pants caught on a branch."

"You left me there," I repeated.

"By the time I got untangled, you were swept away."

"It felt like a hand pushed me down."

"That's your imagination. Those nasty rapids . . . can creep up on you. I forgot."

His voice was phlegmy, and I could barely hear him. After a minute or two, he cleared his throat, gargled, spit out a plume of brown liquid, and said, "Besides, what are you worrying about anyway? Isn't this the Neversink?"

My father and I climbed up a trail to the road, crossed Claussen's Bridge by feet, and walked the beach path to get Francine. She asked me if I was okay and I nodded, wiping the blood from my thighs with a towel and tying it around my waist, sarong-style, to hide the cuts. We packed and went back to the car in silence. I was afraid that if I opened my mouth, all the water from the Neversink would come pouring out and there would be nothing left of me except a skeleton in the shape of a huge fish.

•   •   •

From the front lawn, I heard the squeaking and clunking of the Futterman's Cadillac before I saw its quadruple headlights back down our broken-cement driveway. Francine and I were squeezed together on the hammock, our behinds squished into the sagging diamond-shaped woven rope. Moving my elbows to turn, I upset our balance, and we tumbled to the ground, luckily landing on a soft bed of oak leaves. We brushed ourselves off and stood, facing the driveway where Laura was still waving at the dwindling black phantom. If my father were there and in a good mood, he would have said, as he did whenever he saw the Futtermans in their car, "Where do they think they're going, to a funeral?" Instead, he was in the house, surely in the bedroom with the shades drawn to darkness.

"My cousins just left," Laura said, walking toward us. "Maybe we can all play Family now."

"Not now," I said. I no longer yearned for the three of us to do anything.

"I have to tell you something that Janie said." Laura's hazel eyes sparkled.

That was the last thing I wanted to hear, some pearls of wisdom from Laura's precious cousin. "Not now," I said again.

"But, Mandy." Laura yanked my sleeve as if she wanted to pull me aside. "It's about Benny," she said, whispering into my ear.

I didn't believe her. Laura just wanted to get my attention. I knew her tricks. Without thinking, I said, "Okay, Laura, what is it?" I was ready to call her out.

"Do you want me to walk away?" Francine asked. "I mean if this is private."

"I have no secrets from *you*," I said.

"Well, here goes," Laura said. "Wait until you hear this. Janie said that Benny was our fathers' older brother and that he drowned in the Neversink River when he was a young man. I mean, on purpose. He jumped off the bridge."

"No," I said. "How would Janie know such a thing?"

"She said everybody knew."

I was relieved when Laura's mother called her inside; I didn't want to hear anymore. For the rest of the afternoon, Francine and I stayed in the Sun House. I think we both wanted the Nederlanders to come get her, but something stopped us from saying anything.

"Sorry, I was a scaredy-cat about crossing that rock," she said.

"You weren't," I lied.

"Maybe next time." Francine sniffled after another sneeze. "I guess I'm allergic to a lot of things in the country."

"I guess." It was hard for me to think of something good about this day. I didn't want Francine to go home without having fun. I didn't want her to hate the country, my country. But my eyes felt heavy, and all I wanted to do was sleep.

"Did you want to talk about what Laura said?" Francine asked.

"Not really," I said. "She makes up a lot of stories." And then I thought about my own stories and added, "But with hers, you don't always know they're pretend."

• • • •

By dinnertime, Francine's parents came, and they got in their car. I followed them down the driveway and watched them maneuver the bend toward the village. As I walked up the driveway, Laura came to the front of the house and called to me, "Mandy, it's time for dinner. Your mother wants you inside." I crossed over to the lawn and caught up with my cousin.

"So, I guess Francine won't be coming for another visit," Laura said. "She didn't seem to like the country too much."

"She did so."

"I thought she kept sneezing with all the grass and stuff."

"She did, but she still liked it here. And how was your visit with *your* cousins?"

"It was great. Mandy, maybe you should just be friends with Francine on your block where she doesn't get sick."

"I can be friends with Francine anywhere! You don't get to tell me where I should or where I shouldn't."

That just came out of my mouth. I mean, I didn't think about it too much until Laura got me started. But it made me feel a lot better about things—about Francine looking like Rudolf the red-nosed reindeer; about Laura's broken paddle; about Lester and the Ratner dogs; about my father's eyes, so dark and wild when we were sitting on the grass after I almost drowned.

SHUTOUT

My father was a man of limited tastes, but when he loved something, there was no limit. Above all, my father loved baseball. He loved the New York teams—the Brooklyn Dodgers, Giants, and Yankees. Though I can't remember him going to any stadium—possibly he went to Ebbets Field—he listened to the radio all summer as the announcers spewed batting averages, earned run averages, runs batted in, shutouts, homers, and records for anything that happened more than once. For a nonintellectual sport that had little action, baseball depended on its fans to be obsessive statisticians, giving them something to argue about during the long hours of crotch scratching and tobacco juice spitting.

My father's second love was cigars of all types, ones with shiny gold paper rings that I wore on my fingers for a few minutes until the seal broke or it slid off. His mainstays were Dutch Masters, each wrapped in cellophane and lined in a wooden box like slender sticks of dynamite. His other favorites were untapered Phillies cheroots that came squeezed in a pack until he discovered an uglier version, Italian stogies, short, dark, venous sticks that he would suck on until blackish-brown juice seeped down his fat, ruddy cheeks. Cigars were a permanent part of his facial features, protruding from his shut lips in every photo, staining his teeth a green umber, and imbuing his being with a woody, stinky odor.

I don't remember when I learned that if I wanted to have anything to do with my father, I had to hand him a cigar and the *New York Post* sports pages, which I would scan in advance for baseball trivia to offer in my planned "spontaneous" conversations. That is why when I heard about spring tryouts for the new 1956 girls' baseball team and that the games were played at the local high-school field, blocks from our Flatbush apartment, and that a father could sit in the bleachers and smoke his head off, I had to go. The ages ranged from 9-12, and I was ten and the shortest girl in my class. I was a pretty good ballplayer, though, at least the best thrower and catcher of a pink, rubber Spalding ball on East 22nd Street, the best among my friends on the block whom, I admit, were no great sportswomen.

On the day of the tryouts, I didn't tell anyone. The baseball they handed me was harder and heavier than my Spalding, and I was terrified when the coach lent me a glove and threw a fastball. My hand stung even with the glove, but I was happy to catch the ball, though I soon dropped it. When it was time to bat, I missed each time until the coach inched closer and practically laid the ball on my bat. I tapped it lightly; the ball didn't even make it to the foul line. I knew the coach felt sorry for me because he said, "You can be the water girl, and when the catcher is sick, you can fill in." I didn't care. The important thing was that I got a bright gold-orange baseball cap with black letters, and a matching tee shirt with a black stripe encircling the arms and the numeral six on the back. I sprinted home, took out the iron and pressed my tee shirt, folding it into a neat package as if it came straight from the sports store's shelves.

When my father came home, I ran to the door. "Guess what, Daddy?" I said. As usual, he didn't respond, and after going to pee, he got a bottle of Schlitz from the refrigerator, plopped on his faded brown lounger, and flipped over his *New York Post* to the sports page.

I went to my room and returned, all spiffed up, "Taa-da," I said, wearing my new shirt and cap. "Look, Daddy, I joined the baseball team."

"That so?" he said, looking up for a second.

"My first game is Saturday at eleven, at the high school. Can you come?"

He didn't answer, but he didn't say no so there was hope.

The next day, I heard my mother shouting at him behind their bedroom door. "You'd better say yes," she screamed. "She'll be impossible to live with if you don't go."

• • •

That Saturday, I went to the game a half hour early for batting practice even though I knew the chance of me playing was slim. I filled up the big pitcher with water from the high-school gym and lined up the plastic cups on the table by the field. I also slung a towel over my arm just in case any player needed to wipe her mouth after drinking. During the innings, I sat on the bench ready to play.

Every few minutes, I scanned the bleachers looking for my father among the other dads. I paced a few steps in each direction, searching for the chubby face often mistaken for the gangster actor Edward G. Robinson, pressed against the chained link fence, his stogie popping through.

Somewhere there surely would be a father looking for his daughter, the new water girl. But not that day.

The night before my next game, I draped my baseball tee shirt over the headrest of my father's lounger, hoping that the material would seep into his head as he leaned back dreaming about Jackie Robinson's latest homer. The next morning the shirt was still on the chair, a bit rumpled; the *New York Post* folded over it like a Chinese collapsible straw hat. In the kitchen, as I packed a bologna sandwich in my *Lone Ranger* lunch box, I heard my mother yelling from the living room.

"Amanda, you left your tee shirt on your father's chair."

"I know," I screamed back.

"Put it back in your room where it belongs."

*   *   *

By the end of the season, I played once and struck out, but I caught two fly balls. Though I was constantly on the lookout, my father never came. I realized that if I expected my father to have the slightest interest in my life, I had as much chance as getting a home run with bases loaded. So, I washed and ironed my tee shirt, folded it properly, and laid it in my bottom dresser drawer, never to wear it again.

THE FACTORY

"Would you girls like to go for a ride?" my father asked, standing by my bedroom door, on a Saturday morning in May. Francine and I, who were polishing each other's nails, looked up at him like he had just offered us the chance to be on *Queen for a Day.*

"Go where?" I asked, still in shock. My father never took us anywhere on the weekend, except occasionally to visit my grandmother or Laura, who was nine, a year younger than me.

"It's a surprise," he said.

"What should I tell my parents?" Francine asked.

"Tell them we're going to my factory to pick up some sweaters."

"Really, the factory?" I asked, eagerly. "Oh, Francine, it's so much fun there. We can see all the machines spinning the wool."

"Today's Saturday," my father said. "No one's working. The machines are shut down."

"Then why are we going?"

"I have to go there for something. And while I'm there, you can sift through a big table with sweaters and hats and knitted belts."

"But it's getting hot out, too hot for sweaters."

"Dummy, you'll need them next year."

"Why can't we come back when the weather gets cooler and choose the sweaters then?"

"These are extras, that's why. Do you or don't you want them?"

"We do, we do."

"But Daddy," I said. "I have to be at my baseball game this afternoon."

"What time?"

"At 2:00 as usual."

"You'll get there in plenty of time. And if you miss a game, it won't be the end of the world."

I hated to be late for anything, but I was too excited to worry much.

On the way to the factory in downtown Brooklyn, we picked up Laura and Uncle Sol. We three girls squeezed in the back seat, giggling and gossiping about the factory and its top-1956 seller—the white-angora, dressy sweater with two rows of tiny white beads bordering the rounded collar like a double-strand necklace of cultured pearls. I was so happy pressed together with my closest friend and cousin, on the way to the magical place where my father was like a big-shot director of an animated movie, making sure that tapered steel arms were bending and rising, transforming wispy cotton threads into white torsos.

I had been to the factory twice. Once when I was in kindergarten, my mother took me there after school to bring my father some important papers; the other time, I was in the second grade, and we were doing a unit in manufacturing. My teacher, Mrs. Harrison, asked my father if he could give the class a tour. In his Brooklyn Dodgers cap, he had looked chunky but solid, and a boy named Melvin Steinberg told me, "Your father looks like that actor, what's his name?"

I answered, "I know, Edward G. Robinson."

During the class tour, my father didn't smoke but displayed his cigar in his shirt pocket. He gave every kid a scarf and a carton of orange juice. They wrote him a thank-you note, and I kept them all in an old cigar box where I keep my treasures.

At Gerber's Knitting Mills, my father and uncle unlocked and lifted a gray, corrugated metal wall that protected the entrance. The musty storefront office was jammed with opened cartons of fabric samples; boxes with gold sailor buttons; and packets of elastic binding, the ends draping the floor like rubbery snakes.

We wound our way through the clutter to the open freight elevator, which creaked up two flights into the factory. The huge room was dark, except for a rectangle of light shining through the window at the other end near the sewing tables. My father pulled a dangling yellow string, and a single light bulb illuminated the switch command unit.

"No one's here?" I whispered, remembering the shrieking of orders over the thrumming and clanking of machines in motion.

"Just us," my father said, in a clipped voice.

"Can you turn on the machines so Francine can see?"

"No, Mandy, you need to have people at their stations."

As far as I could see, the arms of the mechanical threaders were folded and clasped like tired old men huddled over their newspapers. My father led us to the sewing tables. The last time I was here, the tables were clear except for neatly piled skeins of wool, twisted and braided like loaves of challah. Now, they were strewn with sweaters of every shape and color like the picked-over remnants at John's Bargain Store at the end of a sale day.

"Aachoo!"

"Bless you, Francine," I said softly, afraid that if I spoke in a normal voice, I would wake somebody hiding in the darkened back-room office.

"It's dusty in here," Laura said, lifting her pigtails to wipe her neck.

"Girls, we have some work to do. In the meantime, go through all this," my uncle said.

"Shouldn't we leave some for you to sell?" Laura asked.

"Don't worry about that now. Choose what you want."

While the men went into the office, we plunged in our hands.

"This is nice," Francine said, fingering a red-and-gray boatneck. "What do you think?" She held it up against her chest, wriggling her reddened pug nose.

"Take it," I said. "It goes with your felt skirt."

"I don't know. This cable-knit with the lace is also pretty." Francine always went after the most feminine styles.

With so many sweaters, not one of us could decide. We tossed them back and forth, asking for opinions. Soon, knitted arms and chests were diving across the table like an army of headless dancing mannequins.

"What are you girls doing?" Sol yelled from the back room.

"Nothing, Daddy," Laura screamed, then lowered her voice. "We'd better make up our minds or my father will be mad."

We poked through the piles some more, and each of us chose two sweaters. I picked two short-sleeved fine knits, one in white and the other in blue. They seemed to match anything. Most of the others were too grown-up for my taste, but I took two of the fancy ones for my sister, Brenda.

Laura selected a blue tweed with a shawl collar and a cardigan with a scooped neck. Both were too big and sophisticated for her, but she insisted she would wear them. She moved to another table piled with accessories. Francine found a brown floppy hat; Laura wrapped a white scarf around her neck like she was Marilyn Monroe; and I chose black knee socks.

The men left the back room and gave us brown paper bags for our stuff. My father had a large ledger book under his arm, and my uncle carried a small metal box with a combination lock.

"There's your hat," I said to my father, pointing to his Brooklyn Dodgers cap, hanging from a nail on the wall. "Why don't you wear it like you always do when you go to work?"

"I must have left it here last week. If you want, take it."

"You mean just to wear for the weekend?"

"No, I mean home, home for good."

"But, why?"

"Stop questioning everything, Mandy!" my father yelled. "Either take it or leave it, it's all the same to me."

It was bad enough my father called me "dummy" in front of Francine, now he was scolding me as if I were a baby. I could feel crying coming, but I held it in. I was good at that.

"Mandy, I think your father's giving you the cap," Francine whispered.

"No, it's his." I lifted it off the nail and held the inside of the cap to my nose. I could smell Brylcreem and Bering cigars—a hatful of my father in the dark-blue globe.

My father pulled the string four times until the light went off, and we took the elevator down and put our bags in the car. Then we went across the street to Angelo's Italian Restaurant, the place my father visited every day for lunch and for a drink after work.

"Bill, Sol, what are you doing here on a Saturday?" called a white-haired man behind the bar.

"Hey, Angelo! We brought some pretty girls to brighten up the joint."

"Is she your youngest?" Angelo asked my father, looking at me.

"Yeah, that's her, the one between the two girls."

"They're all so beautiful, and they look like sisters. But you can tell she's yours, Bill. She has your puppy dog eyes."

"Poor kid."

"And you, Solly?"

"That's my oldest, Laura, with the pigtails."

"Mamma mia, another beauty. How did such ugly brothers wind up with such glamour girls?" Angelo winked at me.

"Rosemary," Angelo called toward the dining room, "come, the Gerber brothers are here. Now boys, what'll you drink—on the house, of course? Girls go sit at the booth. The waitress Rosemary will be over to take your order."

A blonde-haired woman, with a tight black sweater hugging huge boobs, and a black waist apron, ambled into the bar area and stood between my father and uncle, an arm slung around the shoulders of each man. She ran her fingers through the back of my father's greasy hair and said something in his ear that made him laugh. I guessed they were telling dirty jokes from the way they were slapping each other's backs, talking real low, and looking back at us.

Rosemary left the men drinking from glass beer mugs and came to our booth in the back of the restaurant, carrying a brown tray with Cokes and straws. "The Great Pretender" by the Platters played on the gleaming-gold jukebox in the corner, and we hummed along.

"Which one is Bill's little girl?" she asked, putting the drinks on the table.

"Me," I said.

"And I'm Sol's daughter," Laura said.

"How nice . . . what would you girls want to eat? Maybe spaghetti and meatballs? Angelo makes the best meatballs. Or maybe, you'd like to share a pizza?"

"I don't know, what do you want?" I asked the others.

"I don't care," Francine said.

"Just bring them a pie," my uncle yelled.

Two big men, dressed in checked, flannel shirts and Levis, entered the restaurant and walked over to the bar. The taller and fatter one patted my father on the back and sat on the stool next to him. The other man stood behind my uncle. They were all laughing and smoking cigars. It seemed that everyone in the restaurant knew the Gerber brothers, especially my father.

I had never seen my father so loud and so popular before. The only other places I had seen him relate to others were in the country at the village or at a relative's house where he'd sit alone in a corner, sleeping or mumbling some curse words. Except at my grandmother's Passover Seders when he'd drink too much Manischewitz wine, and my mother would tell him, with lips tight together like a ventriloquist, to lower his voice.

I wondered if Angelo and the men knew my father once wrote poetry. I wondered if they knew he almost finished medical school.

Rosemary returned with a big pizza and separated the slices with a rolling circle cutter. We heard the men singing, "For they're jolly good fellows," to our fathers, and clinking their beer mugs.

"We'll surely miss your daddies," Rosemary said.

"Where're they going?" I asked.

"Why, no place, sweet pea," she said, patting my head. "Hey Bill, didn't you tell the girls?" she screamed across the room and walked back to the bar.

"I think our fathers are moving the factory," I said to Laura.

"I was just thinking the same thing. Where do you think they'll go?"

"I hope this doesn't mean that we have to move also."

"Oh no! Don't say that, Mandy." Francine sounded like she was going to cry.

Finally, my father and uncle drifted to our booth and sank down into the soft leather banquette. I smelled beer and cigars over them. My father belched, and I slouched in my seat.

"Are you moving the factory?" Laura asked her father.

"Not exactly."

"But you're going somewhere," I said. "Rosemary said so." My heart started to pound.

"What does that bleached blonde know?" my father said.

"We're just selling the factory," my uncle said. "We're not moving."

"Why?" I asked, looking straight at my father's baggy olive eyes. He pulled a Swiss army knife from his pants pocket and unfurled the rusty blade. Then he lifted a wrapped cigar from his shirt pocket, slit open the cellophane, and sliced off the tip.

"We had to, to help pay the bills," Sol explained.

"Who will run it?"

"Another man."

"It's called Gerber's Knitting Mills; how can another man own it?"

"He'll change the name or just use our name. It's legal. People do it all the time." Sol's voice was calm.

"What will you both do?" I could feel my throat close, tasting vomit. This time I tugged my father's sleeve. He flipped through the laminated menu as if he didn't know it by heart. I remembered my parents' fight last night. I could hear them from my closed bedroom door. It wasn't the usual put-down stuff. It had something to do with money. "What will *you* do?" I repeated, grabbing the menu from my father's hands.

"We're not sure," Sol said as if I were asking him. "For now, I'll work for Uncle Manny, selling sweaters for him, and your dad will help your uncle Irving run his shoe business."

"Will we ever come to the factory again, or to Angelo's?"

My father spit out a glob of cigar juice in the ashtray. He said, "Angelo, the old wop will always be here."

"Bill, your language!" Sol said.

"I gotta watch what I say now?"

I swallowed hard and asked, "Daddy, why didn't you tell us about the factory before?"

"You think you could have done something about it?"

"No, but . . ." Laura kicked me in the shin. I wanted to yell at her, but I couldn't speak.

"Just eat your pizza," he said, standing and turning his back to us. The brothers returned to the bar.

"At least you're not moving," Francine said to me.

"Whew, thank God," I said, pushing away the paper plate with the pizza slice. The cheese looked like ugly brown ropes. "I'd die if we had to move."

I heard my father shouting, "Hey, Rosemary. Do you want to get some sweaters before it's too late?"

"Yeah, that would be nice. How about it, Angelo?"

"Go ahead. But don't take all day."

By the time my father and Rosemary returned, with two shopping bags stuffed with sweaters and scarves, Francine and Laura finished the pizza. My stomach recovered in time for dessert. Francine ordered the coconut gelato because it sounded "foreign," Laura got chocolate cake and managed to smear a brown blob on her white shirt, and I had a tortoni. I was licking out specks of toasted almond from the rim of the miniature white, accordion paper cup when my uncle said it was time to leave.

We said good-bye to Angelo, Rosemary, and the other men, crossed the street, and hopped into the back seat of the car. My father and uncle closed the factory's metal gate and snapped the lock shut. I sat by the window and opened it all the way. As we drove off, I stuck out my head and strained my neck up toward the factory windows and pictured rows of men and women sitting on tall swivel stools, surrounding the machinery, pulling at horizontal lines of thread, flattening sleeves, untwisting collars, and pushing two arms and a vest under long, tapping needles until they miraculously came through the other end in one piece.

I blinked and then everyone disappeared. All I could see was my father's old Dodgers cap where I had hooked it back in place, hanging by itself from a nail in the wall.

THE ATTIC

It was the kind of up-and-down August country rain that formed instant splashy mud puddles around the pine trees, that chilled the temperature so that we had to wear sweaters under our yellow slickers, that made the air smell like just-mowed grass and just-dug worms and just-cut roses. It was the kind of country rain that felt like it would go on all day; but could also stop suddenly, shimmering the wet green leaves of the sagging apple trees. And, it was the kind of rain that inspired Laura and me to head for Grandma Sarah's room, a compact rectangular space with two single beds, separated by a night table, and two doors that hid terrifying objects.

The near door opened to a narrow closet. Two years ago, when I was eight and Laura was seven, we snooped inside and touched a long hard thing in the corner behind clothes. We ducked under a white terrycloth bathrobe hanging from the closet bar and pulled out what first looked like a dark stick. When we lifted it into the light, we saw it was a shotgun. We gasped, placing it back without saying a word. I was petrified to even touch it, sure that my sweaty fingerprints would be pressed into the shiny brown wood the way a comic book came off on my Silly Putty.

The other door, just past Grandma Sarah's pedal-foot Singer sewing machine, led to the attic. The stairs were high and narrow; we approached each step like trapeze artists, pushing our palms against the side walls for support. As we reached the top, following the brightening trail of light, we bent our heads to keep from banging them on the slanted beamed ceiling. Then we moved into more open space, stood tall, and shook our hands against our shirts, trying to loosen the cobwebs that stuck to our fingers like strands of chewed bubble gum.

I felt like Alice in Wonderland, my body growing bigger and bigger, my hands above me holding back the shrinking ceiling from squashing me together as if I were the insides of a sandwich. Gray light filtered in from two small arched windows at the far end of the long, cavernous space. When it was sunny, those windows flashed misty tubes of white speckled dust across the room. But now with the rainstorm outside, the attic was dark, and it took a few seconds for my eyes to get their bearings. I squinted and felt a wave of musty heat like I was trapped inside a giant airless hope chest. My nose filled with the smells of faded green army blankets and a yellowed wedding trousseau pressed between mothballs.

Near the windows, slats of dim light on the wood floor were spotted with pointed, starry shapes. I knew what they were—the clawed feet of stuffed birds mounted on metal pedestals. Depending on how the light shone, we could make out different features of these horrible creatures: a rust feathered rooster, with a pointed quill of a beak and tiny black eyes; a black, hawk-like bird, its neck and wings hunched like an old witch frozen on her broom. The more I stared at the attic's corners, the more I imagined rows of beady black eyes watching, daring us to move—monster birds preparing to pounce and peck at our skin.

"I hate those awful birds," I whispered, unsure if they could hear me.

"Me too. I can't believe Grandma Sarah used to have them all over the house."

"She said Grandpa Sam liked to collect stuffed birds."

Suddenly, we heard a squeaking and tapping sound, as if there was one of these creepy birds stuck inside the walls, scratching to get out.

"Oh, my God, I'm going to pee in my pants," Laura said, wheezing. "Let's get out of here quick."

We felt our way along the flat walls to our left, opened a door, and slammed it shut. It was a small square room, taken up by an old lumpy double bed; but to Laura and me it was a wondrous refuge.

"I'll open the window, I can't breathe," I said, ambling around the bed's metal railing. I nudged the window sill, lifted the peeled and creaky frame, and stuck my head out, the cold rain soaking my hair and dripping down my cheeks. I not only saw Siegel's Bungalow Colony but beyond to the treetops of Mountainview's namesake. On a clear day, I could stand by this window and watch the people at Siegel's scurrying in the lawn like squirrels or swimming in the pool like frogs. On those sunny days, I'd feel like Alice in her largest state, looking down on her little animal kingdom.

"Come in from the window. You're getting sopping wet," Laura said.

I stepped back inside the room and scanned for changes since last summer. I was always amazed by the sudden brightness of this room, compared to the dark space of the open attic, and how the light glimmered on the shiny pictures tacked over every inch of the walls. There were large autographed photos of movie stars like Humphrey Bogart and others I didn't know, such as Norma Shearer, Douglas Fairbanks, and Bela

Lugosi. Interspersed, there were pictures of boxers, including Jack Dempsey with his gloved fists high in the air, Maxey Rosenbloom in the ring, and an unrecognizable man whose signature was smudged, sweat all over his face and his mouth swollen like he was trying to swallow a bowl of mashed potatoes.

A big oak dresser stood against one wall of the room. On the top were more photos—this time of real people—in blackened silver frames with velvet cardboard stands. The largest picture was of a child about three years old, with chubby cheeks and long curls, dressed in a white puffy-sleeved shirt and baggy pants that gathered below the knees. I knew this was my uncle Sol because Grandma Sarah told me when I once took the photo downstairs; but before that, I thought it was a little girl.

Next to Sol's photo, framed in a dark-brown cardboard, three-way folder with fancy brown borders was a photo of my father. He wore a double-breasted suit and a striped tie. His hair was combed straight back; his eyes stared out; his full lips smirked. He looked like a mini Al Capone, but he was only thirteen. It was his bar mitzvah picture.

The other furniture in the room was a tall mahogany closet with an old-fashioned rusty key in the keyhole. I turned it and pulled back, opening the closet's two side doors. Hanging on the inside door's hooks were two pairs of black, cracked-leather ice skates. On the closet shelf, there was a pile of old sweaters, five V-necks in different colors. Stacks of large books and boxes of newspaper clippings cluttered the closet floor.

I took out an oversized book, and Laura and I sat on the bed. It was a photo album stuffed with pictures of heavy women, hair parted down the front, and men with starched collars and long coat jackets. They must have been relatives, people my father knew since this had been my father's old room, his sanctuary when he came home from college.

I loved to come up here and run my fingers through all these saved things. Here I learned that my father had been a teenager, that he started smoking cigars in high school, that he had aunts and uncles, that he went ice-skating, that he loved boxing and the movies, and that he was a man who enjoyed glossy pictures of people around him when he slept.

Placing the album aside, I flipped through another book—a large blue one, "Erasmus Hall High School, Brooklyn, New York, 1929." Under my father's picture, it said: "Grow little seedling grow." Then I picked up a brown yearbook from Long Island University and found my father standing with the basketball team in his second year there. He must have been something—a basketball player at five feet six. I found a catalog from Dalhousie University in Nova Scotia, where my father went to study medicine. I just couldn't imagine that this was my father—the man who went nowhere except to work (and Angelo's Italian Restaurant) and the country, who never read anything but the newspaper, who didn't seem to like anyone except for people I didn't know, the man who never uttered a word to me. I couldn't imagine that this man, my father, once had a life!

With the edge of my shirt, I rubbed the yearbooks and catalog back and forth, making sure there were no dust spots before I put them back in the closet.

"Can you believe my father was going to be a doctor?" I asked Laura.

"No, and did you know mine was going to be a lawyer?"

"How do you know?"

"My mother told me that the way I answer her back, I should be a lawyer, like my father was supposed to be."

"Why didn't he?"

"She said he didn't work hard enough, and I should be careful I don't do that in school. Did that happen with your daddy?"

"I once asked my mother, and she said to ask my father. I did, and he wouldn't answer me. Maybe he decided he didn't want to be a doctor."

"I guess they didn't need to know that stuff in the sweater factory. And now, in their new jobs . . . shh. I think I heard something."

"It must be the rain on the garbage cans outside," I said.

A clomping sound, like horses descending wood planks, came from the attic space outside our room. Then it was quiet.

"That was definitely not the rain," Laura said.

Now the clomping was followed by brushing and squeaking as if something metal was being dragged.

"Somebody's here!" I squeezed Laura's hands and held my breath.

"Let's lock the door. I'm not leaving this room," Laura whimpered, scratching at the scabs in her legs.

"It's worse if we're locked in. We have to get out, get to the staircase."

"I can't move. I can't go." Laura started to cry, sniffling and making wailing sounds as if she was going to have one of her tantrums.

"Stop it! He'll hear you and come after us. Hold your hand over your mouth."

"I want my daddy!" Laura sputtered, breathing so hard I was sure whoever was out there had heard us.

Maybe we should open the window, I thought, and climb on the roof and jump down, but that was dangerous since Laura wore those big brown orthopedic shoes. Or maybe we should open the door, slink out behind the cartons and make a dash for the staircase. I was afraid to look at Laura because if I saw her face, I'd also start crying. But since I was the oldest, it was up to me to take over, so I closed my eyes and said to Laura, "Listen Jim, it's me, John."

"What?"

"Come on, let's play John and Jim, but this time we're not in the woods. Pretend we must get away from some mean robbers. Let's tiptoe toward the door. I'll throw this yearbook in the direction of the stuffed birds to make a ruckus. Then we'll make a run for the stairs."

"I can't, Mandy!"

"You can, and I'm John. Now stop being a baby! Remember you're brave, Jim. Follow me, I'll go first."

Laura held onto my shirt so tightly, I could hardly move, but I managed to open the door and take a few steps to the side. "Close the door behind you," I whispered. I didn't want whoever was there to see us in the light.

"But I can't see."

"You can if you look carefully there." I pointed to a horizontal shape in the distance. "I think that's the staircase. When I pinch you, get ready to run that way. Are you ready?"

"Mmm."

"Okay, get set."

We heard a throat-clearing noise. Then a name was echoed. At first, I thought someone was calling "Mandy" but then it sounded more like "sister."

"Mandy, who was that?"

"How would I know?" I turned my head to look across the long space, in the direction of the stuffed birds. I could make out a tall, dark figure standing in the corner, with a flashlight beam coming from him, shining into the little black eyes of one of those hawks. Any second, I expected it to come alive and fly into my face, followed by the flapping wings of hundreds of other wild creatures waking up from the dead.

"Who's there?" I croaked.

We heard faint grunts that sounded like a man's voice.

"Daddy, is that you?" I whispered.

There was no answer.

"Daddy?" I said, louder.

"No, no," we heard.

"Mandy, Mandy, I'm so scared."

"Me too," I said, pinching Laura and dragging her away from the voice, closer to the staircase. Scrunching under sloping beams, we were closer to the roof and the rainstorm rumblings above our heads.

"Here . . . don't be 'fraid," the voice seemed to say.

"Who is it?" I shouted.

As the man answered, it thundered outside, and we couldn't understand all his words. It was something like, "It's me . . . yessir."

"Come run!" I screamed and pulled Laura's hands toward the stairs. We practically fell down the steps and banged into the closed door. I fumbled for the glass handle, turned it, pushed Laura inside my grandmother's room, and slammed the door.

"Help! help!" Laura shouted, by now crying so loudly she sounded like she was choking.

We ran screaming into the hall. Laura went flying into the apron of my grandmother.

"What is it?" Grandma Sarah asked.

"What?" Aunt Virginia yelled, bumping into my grandmother.

"A monster, ther-e was a . . . mon," Laura spluttered.

"There was someone up there . . . in the attic," I said.

"I'm calling the police," my aunt said. "I wouldn't be surprised if this house is haunted."

"Wait a second," Sarah said. "I know who it is."

"Where's your mother?" my aunt asked me.

"She went to Siegel's."

"She's still there?"

"Get a grip on yourself," Sarah said to my aunt. "It's only Lester."

"But we didn't see Lester. It looked like a hairy giant," I said.

Just then, we heard knocking from inside the attic door.

My grandmother stepped into her room.

"No, don't answer it!" I cried.

"The shotgun, I'm getting the gun," my aunt said.

"Oh, no you're not!" my grandmother said. "Just be still all of you."

Aunt Virginia pushed my grandmother aside, and before we knew what was happening, we were all in Grandma Sarah's room staring at my aunt pointing the shotgun toward the attic door.

"I know how this works, don't think I don't," she screamed at the closed door. "And I happen to know it's loaded." She drew the shotgun up to her eyes, cocked it, and put her finger on the trigger. "Girls get back. I'm going to shoot now, you hear me in there?"

"No, Virginia, stop," my grandma said, pulling on my aunt's blouse, trying to get her fingers on the gun's handle. The two women struggled, and a deafening boom went off. Plaster flakes fell on our heads, and there was a huge crater in the ceiling.

"Virginia, you could have shot the girls. Now, give me that gun." My aunt's arm dropped, and my grandmother kicked the shotgun under her bed.

Then Sarah took her daughter-in-law in her arms like she was going to hug her but shook her real hard. "You have to control yourself, you hear," she said in a calmer tone. "You're a mother now. Where did you learn to use that thing and when did you get bullets? How could you keep a loaded weapon in my house with children? What were you thinking?"

"I was thinking about protecting my family from just this kind of thing." Virginia's lips twitched.

"Protecting them from who?"

"With the men away all week, you can't be too careful."

Then Grandma Sarah opened the attic door. There was Lester, our neighbor's handyman, his face very red, with wet dirt smudges on his cheeks, standing tall and skinny. In each hand, he held up a black hawk, each bird frozen in pre-flight mode.

"Lester!" I gasped.

"Lester, now who told you to go up there?" my aunt asked.

"Why the other Misses. Misses Estelle. This here girl's mama."

"I knew *she* had something to do with this."

"What does this have to do with my mother?" I asked.

"Your mother wants to get rid of everything—and everyone—in this house." My aunt's cheeks were pink and shiny with sweat.

"Hold your tongue, Virginia," Grandma Sarah said. "Who do you think you're talking to? Mandy's only a child."

"She should know the truth by now."

"You're always suspecting Estelle of something," my grandmother said. "All Estelle did was ask Lester if he wanted to take those birds, the ones Sam had named after Sol and Bill. The other birds had family names, too. Estelle thought it was time we gave them away, that they were frightening the girls. And I gave Lester permission to go up now. I didn't know the girls were up in Bill's old room."

"You're always defending Estelle," Virginia said.

My grandmother's voice made a sudden switch, from frightened, take-charge mode to fake reasoning with a child tone: "Now girls, go inside and wash up for lunch. Virginia, you'd better check on the baby. Lester, come with me. I'll open the door for you, you have your hands full."

Before I entered the bathroom, I about-faced and watched Lester prance down the hallway. From the back, he looked like a huge flying creature himself. He raised his arms as if he were launching the birds Sol and Bill from their perches, ready to take off over the skies, into the unknown. Their feathers didn't move; they were plastered to their stuffed bodies, as dead as the ancestors in my father's album.

THE SECRET

This was the first summer my family lived in a newly built cottage behind the main house, supported, financially and otherwise, by Grandma Sarah to not only alleviate the crowded conditions in her house but the constant tension between my mother and aunt. It was not much more than a large bungalow with two tiny bedrooms and an open great room, a knotty-pine walled L-shape that included a couch and chairs, dining alcove, and compact galley kitchen. While I was happy to finally have my own room (with Brenda), I missed being under the same roof as Laura; the distance between us sometimes felt as far as the Neversink River.

To make me feel less "homesick," I planned an adventure in the woods. Laura and I told our mothers we were going to visit our neighbor Barbara Siegel; and on the way there, we snuck from the back of Siegel's Bungalow Colony to our wishing well, under the bent-up rusty fence, and uphill through the woods to our rock, where we rested awhile. There, we decided to become our fearless aliases, John and Jim as Indian scouts. From my pocket, I slid out my grandmother's knife-tipped bottle can opener, jumped off our rock, and carved a *J* on the barks of trees beyond Laura's sight, shouting the rules: "Laura, I mean Jim, I'll go ahead, and meanwhile close your eyes. See if you can find me by tracking the *J*s. Then it will be your turn."

Laura leaned facedown on her arms and counted to a hundred. I scooted into a dense area, making my mark on the tallest trees I could find. Soon I heard Laura call, "Ready or not, here I come," and she whooped and hollered every time she found a *J*. A few minutes of silence went by, and I was getting nervous. Then Laura yelled, "John? Oh John?"

"What Jim?"

"Mandy, where are you? I think I'm lost."

Just when I was about to mark my *J* on a giant maple tree, I noticed a break in the bark on the side. Carved in a rectangular space, were uneven capital letters spelling the name BENNY.

"Laura, quick, here," I yelled, coming into the clearing, waving my arms.

"Oh, so far up there?"

"Hurry," I said, "you'll never believe what I just found."

Laura climbed up the slope and followed me into the thicket. I pointed at my discovery.

"Oh my God! Benny."

"Can you believe it?"

This was the second time we had come across this boy's name in writing. Last summer when I was nine, Laura and I had been helping Grandma Sarah keep score for her gin rummy game with her two grandmother cronies. Laura had flipped the pages in the wrinkled brown pad that Sarah used to record the scores, and in the back was a page with three columns of numbers in smeared blue ink. The names at the top of the columns were our fathers' Bill and Sol, and then came Benny. When I had asked who Benny was, all three grandmas froze as if I had announced the name on a Nazi death list. Later that summer, Laura's cousin Janie said she heard that Benny was my father's brother and that he had killed himself in the river. The next time we saw Janie, she admitted she could have misunderstood her parents talking and was no longer sure of what she had heard.

"Benny," I said to Laura in the woods. "Who could he be?"

"I wish I knew."

By now we were on top of a slope. "Let's go a little farther," I said. "I can see light through the woods. It must be another clearing. Let's find out where it goes."

"I don't know," Laura said. "Maybe we're going too far away."

"Five more minutes," I said.

Laura and I wove through the trees and brush, slashing our arms like machetes to clear overhanging branches from our faces. On another thick tree, again we saw Benny's name, this time carved in a broken-lettered script. Soon, we came to a treeless area bordered by a high wire-and-beam fence. We followed the fence to the right until we reached an open wood gate.

"Look, let's go through," I said. Past the fence, there was a field of high grass with mounds of fly-encircling wet dung. "Ugh, I almost stepped in it," I said. "I hope we don't bump into some wild animals."

•　　　•　　　•

"Mandy, I'm scared. We should go back. Wait, I think I see a building."

Up ahead, there was a long, low shack. In the yard, there must have been fifty hens and roosters flapping and clucking away, darting in and out of the shack's door. We leaned against the chicken-wire fence surrounding the periphery, pressing hexagonal imprints into our faces, mesmerized by the prancing birds, while spitting white and rust feathers from between our lips. A beautiful collie like Lassie ran into us, sniffing between our legs, his tail whipping our knees like a whisk broom. The dog circled us and barked as if he wanted to lead us somewhere, so we stumbled behind him, down a mound leading to a large, red-brown barn.

We followed the dog inside, where it smelled like manure, hay, and leather saddles. We heard horses whinnying, sneezing, swishing air through their cheeks, and the clanking of their metal shoes kicking against the wood stalls. As we moved closer to the horses, an old man in overalls holding a big wooden bucket approached.

"Hi," he said softly.

"Hi. Sorry, we just walked in," I said.

"That's okay. Where did you girls come from? Didn't see no car pull up."

"We came from the woods," I said, "from our house, way down there."

"Where do you live?"

"The brown houses on River Road, between Siegel's and Ratner's."

"All the way from River Road?"

"Yes."

"Why, that's pretty darn far. You must be tired."

"Not really, we rested."

"What's your names?"

"Mandy and Laura Gerber."

"Oh, I knowed your folks, the Gerbers, yeah. Give them my regards."

"What's your name?"

"Hadley. Tell them the farmer near the stables. Farmer Hadley, they'd know me."

•　　　•　　　•

For the next week or so, we went to the farm every chance we got. Farmer Hadley showed us how to brush the horses, feed the cows, and collect eggs. He even took us on a hayride around the farm and through the fields. And he told us we were welcome any time, that it was a pleasure to get a surprise visit from the Gerber cousins. We never mentioned that we didn't tell our parents about seeing him. We always said they sent their best, figuring that he would be upset to know we came without permission.

On our fourth visit, when Farmer Hadley was gathering hay in the barn, I took a deep breath. Laura and I had decided that this was the day.

"Can I ask you a question?" I said. Laura stood at my side.

"Shoot."

"Well, did you ever know a man or a boy named Benny?"

Farmer Hadley leaned his pitchfork against the wall and faced us. His eyes were strained and squinty, a look I had seen on other adults many times.

"Why do you ask?"

"We've found his name on two trees in the woods. The second tree was not far from the farm."

"Yeah, Benny used to come here."

"He did?" Laura shouted.

"Oh, a lot in them days. Fine young man. Used to bring a puppy dog sometimes or his rifle. He liked to go shooting."

"What did he look like?" I asked.

"Nice enough looking, tall. I remember he had the clearest blue eyes you ever seen. They looked right through a person."

"Did he ever come with anyone else?" Laura asked.

"Let me see. No. No one. No one, except, of course, his brothers that last time."

"Brothers?" I asked.

"Yeah, you know, your daddies."

I felt the blood drain from my head and flopped into a pile of hay. It was the same way I felt when I had terrible pouring nosebleeds at school—part of me terrified of not knowing what was going to happen and the other part sure that it was going to happen the same way it always did.

Maybe Laura was also shocked and not shocked by the news. She looked pale, but she'd looked a lot worse after a fight with her mother.

It took us a few minutes to get over the news and pretend we were okay. As we were about to say good-bye, I said to Farmer Hadley, "Can I ask you one more thing?"

"You won't faint, will you?"

"No, I promise."

"Okay."

"Do you know whatever happened to Benny?"

"You mean you don't?"

"Well, we do, but we don't."

"I can't say then. Better to ask your daddies. All I can say is it was a shame. A darn, stinking shame."

"Brothers!" I said to Laura as we rested on our rock.

"Brothers, I can't believe it. I didn't believe it when Janie said it. It's just not possible. We would have known. Someone else would have told us."

"Why would Farmer Hadley lie to us?"

"Would you rather believe our parents, grandma, and just about everybody else lied to us?" Laura said.

"No, but . . . I don't know. None of this makes any sense. If Benny is our uncle, why are they keeping him a secret? You think he's some kind of criminal?"

"What could he have done?" she asked.

Farmer Hadley gave us the evidence we needed that Benny was one of our own. Now that we had this knowledge, we didn't know what to do with it.

• • •

On the second Saturday after we found the farm, Uncle Sol drove us to a pizza restaurant on the road to Fallsburg. On the left side, we saw a sign that said Hadley's Farm and Stables.

I asked my uncle, "Where are the stables?"

He said, "About a mile or so down that road," pointing to a dirt path under the sign.

I didn't want to get Laura in trouble by telling her father we had gone all the way in the woods to the farm, so I was careful. "Did you ever go to the farm?" I asked.

"Maybe once or twice."

"With who?"

"My brother."

"Your brother? Like who?"

"What do you mean, like who? Your father Mandy, who else?"

"How far are we now from our house?"

"Oh, let's see, maybe five miles to town, and then another mile."

When I added it together, I realized that the farm was at least seven miles away from our house by car. But it took us almost the same time to get to the farm through the woods as it took to walk to town, which was a mile away. And that night, lying in my bed, I couldn't stop thinking about it. When Laura and I climbed behind our house, past our rock, up a hill, through a fence to the farm, we came out at the other end of Mountainview's outskirts, bypassing town. We didn't amble round and round like a swirl of marble frosting on the cover of a Betty Crocker cake mix box; we sliced right through the countryside like a knife.

When I was a lot younger and went to Brighton Beach with my best friend, Francine, we'd dig deep into the dark wet sand by the surf, filling our blue-and-yellow plastic pails, turning them over into packed mounds that we made into castles with moats and winding paths and secret passageways. One time, Francine's father came over to warn us that the tide was changing and that our castle city might be swept away. We scooped out more trenches so that the foaming saltwater would settle into little rivers, rushing through our handmade mazes. We kept digging and digging, trying to trap the water, when Francine's father said, "You'll dig so far down, you'll reach China."

For years, I carried that knowledge with me, like the North Pole whereabouts of Santa Claus. At first, I believed that, since the world was round, if we were on one side, then it made sense that someone else was on the other as if all people just sat on the edges of a globe. Now, if China was on the other side of the world, then it made sense that we could reach China by burrowing through the insides of the earth like a gopher. If Brighton Beach was the direct opposite of the Chinese wall, then all we needed was an extra-long tunnel; and maybe if an American dug real deep from one side and a Chinese dug from the other, the two could touch hands, American to Chinese.

But this year, 1956, as we cut a direct path across miles of the Catskill Mountains to get to a magical farm with all kinds of animals and a kindly old farmer, I began to wonder if by some miracle God was trying to get us to Benny.

•　•　•

My mother once said that when she was pregnant with Brenda, it seemed that every woman she saw in the street was pregnant. Then she explained that when you are suddenly aware of something, you see things you hadn't noticed before. This was how it was with Benny.

We shared our Benny clues with our neighbor Barbara Siegel. Halfway between my age and Laura's, Barbara always wanted to play with us. She didn't have many friends at the bungalow colony, maybe because she was the granddaughter of the owner and maybe because she was pudgy, wore glasses, and was nosy. When we had told her about Benny, she promised to poke around and ask questions from the more elderly renters. Days afterward, she knocked on my bedroom window at eight in the morning, and I slipped out the front door to meet her. We stopped at the Sun House gazebo and sat on the swinging couch.

"Listen Mandy, I couldn't wait to tell you what I found."

"What?"

"I'm not so sure, Mandy, maybe I shouldn't give it to you."

"What?" My heart was pounding.

"I found this in an old scrapbook that my grandfather had in the storage room," Barbara said, reaching into her pocket and handing me a folded newspaper clipping. I opened it and saw the headline, "Local Boy Jumps to Death." My breath caught in my throat. I read on:

> Benjamin J. Gerber, 22, eldest son of Sam and Sarah Gerber of River Road, was found dead in the Neversink River on August 22. Earlier that day, Benjamin tried to hang himself from a tree in the woods near the Hadley Farm. Around his neck was a dog's leash. His younger brothers, William, 20, and Solomon, 16, found his body in time to revive him. On their way home, William stopped his car by Claussen's Bridge to let another car pass. Benjamin got out of the back seat, climbed onto the bridge, and jumped to his death.
>
> Benjamin had been on leave from Sullivan State Mental Asylum. The death was ruled an apparent suicide.

I sat immobile for a while with the newspaper article folded on my lap. Without thanking Barbara, I trudged into my cottage. My mother was standing by the kitchen sink.

"I *know* you know something," I said.

My mother sucked in her breath. "You startled me, Mandy. I didn't see you come in. What do I know?"

"You must know something important about my uncle."

"Sol is outside now. I can hear him mowing the lawn."

"Not Sol. Benny. You know, the one who killed himself. The one who doesn't seem to exist. The one nobody in this family ever talks about."

My mother tapped out a cigarette from a pack lying on the counter. Her hand was shaking so, she had trouble lighting the match. Finally, she took a deep drag before speaking. "How did you find out?"

"Barbara Siegel gave me an old newspaper clipping. Tell me."

"It wasn't my idea not to tell you. If you read an article about it, you must know."

"Was Benny crazy?"

"This is not for me to say."

"Why not? You are always reading your psychology books. And Daddy says you think everyone in the family has some mental illness."

"You don't have to quote your father to me."

"Mommy, I want to know about Benny. Please."

"Okay, I think he was okay growing up, maybe a little sensitive I heard. Then he had a breakdown, a fit. They had to take him to a mental hospital. They thought he was getting better, and he started to come home on visits. Nobody knows much more."

"Why doesn't anyone talk about him?"

"Some people, especially your grandparents' generation, are ashamed of mental illness. Also, it's hard to deal with suicide. Everyone feels guilty, and everyone blames everybody else."

"I hate secrets."

"Your father and uncle Sol found him sprawled on a cliff in the river."

"But it wasn't their fault."

"Apparently, your grandfather had asked your father to keep an eye on Benny, not to let him out of his sight. Your father promised, but I guess he got sidetracked at the farm and Benny wandered off. Later, he stopped the car by the bridge because of an oncoming car, and Sol had to pee, and in a split-second, Benny got out and jumped."

"Daddy must have suffered so much."

"Yes."

"Does anyone know why Benny killed himself?"

"I had heard that his beloved dog, one related to the Ratner dogs, had died that morning. Benny was very upset. But that hardly explains suicide."

My mother held a cup of coffee and sat with a thud. Her cheeks were fresh and smooth and pink; the whites around her slitty brown eyes were clouded over with cigarette smoke. She looked like a teenager who had stayed up all night.

I thought of the many hidden twists and turns that people have in their lives. My father shuffled to the bathroom and flushed the toilet.

"Well, I guess your father's up," my mother said. "When he comes in, why don't you give him a hug or a kiss?"

"I don't want to. I hate when you ask me."

"If I can't ask *you*, who can I ask?"

"Anyone else."

"You know Amanda, he needs his family so. You're a big girl now. You have to be the one to go to him."

I wanted to run to my room and slam the door shut; instead, I went to my father, who was sitting now in his favorite brown lounge chair lighting a cigar. I put my arms around his neck and kissed him on his cheek. He shook his face.

"Did Sol bring us the paper yet? He was supposed to leave it outside the door when he finished," he said.

"I'll check the doormat." I brought back the newspaper and handed it to him. Standing behind his chair, I watched him turn the pages, waiting for him to say thanks. I stared at his scraggly hairline, focusing on an ugly black mole on his neck. Had I noticed it before? As my eyes bore into his scalp, I silently commanded him to about-face, and for once make the first move. I waited.

My father sifted through the paper until he got to his puzzle. He lifted a pencil from his shirt pocket and filled in a few numbers.

"Good puzzle?" I asked, but my father didn't answer. If he doesn't drop that pencil, turn around, and acknowledge me in three seconds, I vowed, I'll grab the paper and hit him over the head. Hit him over and over until I hear his voice, until he tells me to stop. Just when I was about to lift my arm, I remembered my mother's words. It was up to me, she had said. He was in a delicate state. What if I said something wrong and he went over the edge? It would be my fault.

Then everything I learned about Benny began to swirl around my head like a tiny tornado of snow. I felt as if I could reach up and gather the gauzy secrets, pack a snowball, and throw it out my window to form a face, the face of my dead uncle, Benny. In that instant, I knew I had nothing more to lose. Nothing could be worse than silence.

"Daddy," I said, my voice louder than I expected. There was no answer.

"Daddy, I know all about Benny."

My father dropped his pencil to the floor.

"Did you hear me, Daddy? I said I know about your brother Benny."

The only sound I could hear came from inside my chest. I ran to my room.

Nameless, my matted, stuffed black-and-white dog was lying on my pillow, on the same spot every day since my father had bought her for me when I was five years old. I gathered Nameless in my arms, pressing her flat underbelly to my chest. Her insides were stuck in clumps, visible through the opened stitches along her stomach.

"Nameless," I sobbed. "You are my witness. I will never, ever hide from the truth, as long as I live." As I squeezed her, my breast poked her inside rubber horn, and she squeaked. In her own way, my stuffed animal answered me as my father never could.

THE DELIVERY GIRL

I was still in bed when the phone shrilled from the kitchen of our new cottage. This was the first time I heard the ring of our sunburst-yellow wall phone, and it seemed to shake the foundation like a mild earthquake.

"Anyone getting it?" My mother yelled. I heard her stumbling outside my door.

"Let it ring," my father said. His voice was distant, from the direction of the living-room area.

I got out of bed and banged into my mother in the hall.

"Who can it be?" she asked, groggily.

"Who cares?" my father said, already sitting in his chair.

"Why didn't you get it?" my mother asked him.

"What for? It can't be good news at this hour."

"What time is it?" I asked

"A little past eight." My mother picked up the phone. "Too late," she said. "There's a dial tone."

A few minutes later, there was a knock at the door, and it was Grandma Sarah.

"What is it Ma?" my father asked.

"The phone. I got it."

We shared a party line. I loved that our number was Mountainview 9 as if we were among a small group of special people.

"It was Brenda," my grandmother added.

"Brenda?" My mother asked, with alarm. "Where is she? What's wrong?"

"Relax, nothing to worry about. She just got to Shady Grove, at the camp house and realized she forgot her bathing suit, the blue one. She's with her group. She wants to know if Mandy can bring it to her before ten when she takes the girls for a morning swim. She left it hanging in the bathroom."

"Okay, I'll go," I said.

"You'd better go now while you know where Brenda is. She may take the girls somewhere."

I didn't question my grandmother's logic. At a small hotel, it was difficult to get lost with a pack of second graders.

"I have blintzes made," Grandma said. "Sol went to the village for fresh rolls, and Estelle, there's fresh coffee. Come over for breakfast."

"Fresh, fresh? Well, I hate it when my rolls and coffee talk back to me," my father said.

"Oh Bill," my mother teased. It was a rare moment of tenderness between my parents, especially before their first cup of coffee.

• • • •

I wriggled into my bathing suit, hoping that the pool would be unoccupied and I could take a quick swim. We didn't use Shady Grove's pool often because my grandma reminded us that we weren't paying guests and she would be embarrassed as she knew the owners for years. But Laura and I snuck there whenever we could. It was a small pool, but it had a non-scary, low-height diving board and I was getting good at my swan dives. Now that Brenda was a counselor at Shady Grove, I felt a little freer about using the pool, though my sister warned me that she could lose her job if I hung around too much. So, I slipped into a green-striped sunsuit that hid my bathing suit.

On the way, I stopped by Grandma Sarah's and lifted a blintz from a platter on the kitchen table, squeezing and sucking out the cottage cheese as I skipped down the driveway and trotted toward the camp house, near the lake across the road from Shady Grove's main building.

Brenda and her girls were sitting outside on oversized picnic tables working on papier-mâché clowns.

When I handed Brenda the paper bag with her bathing suit, she hugged me. If that wasn't miraculous enough, she said, "Hey girls, I'd like you to meet my sister, Mandy." They looked up from their work and politely smiled. I waved. So far, this day was turning into a nice family experience.

I trudged up Shady Grove's driveway and turned toward the pool. Bruce, the lifeguard, Brenda's one and only, was bending in his tight black Speedo trunks, grazing the water's surface with a leaf skimmer. He was about 5 feet 10 inches and had bulging shoulder and arm muscles. His dirty-blond hair was combed back, glistening with moisture.

I opened the wrought-iron gate.

"Hi Mandy, what are you doing here at this hour?"

"I had to bring Brenda her bathing suit. She left it home."

"Oh, you're a good sister."

"Today I am. Can I take a quick swim, I mean when you're finished cleaning?"

"Sure, go ahead. I can finish later."

I jiggled out of my sunsuit and headed for the deep end. I climbed the two steps of the diving board ladder. With measured paces to the edge, I straightened my legs, positioning my toes so that they curled slightly over the edge of the board, bent my knees, arched my back, stretched my arms out from the sides and then brought them together over my head as I sprung forward. I didn't jump too high as I was terrified of losing control in the air, but I managed enough leverage to slice in cleanly and avoid a belly flop. I quickly emerged from the pool, wiggled off the water, and resumed my diving stance.

"That was great," Bruce called, clapping. "Next time, spring a little higher."

I did as Bruce instructed and dove in deeper and cleaner. I followed with two more dives and felt a little guilty for showing off in front of my sister's movie-star-handsome almost-boyfriend.

Holding my sunsuit over my arms as I dripped, I said thanks and bye to Bruce and aimed toward the shortcut through the shuffleboard court and the outdoor dining tables. Behind me, I heard a voice. That voice.

"Hey, I'd recognize that mushy tushy anywhere."

I didn't turn to face the speaker, my father's friend Leon, the man I hated more than anyone in the world. My heartbeat hammered my chest; my breath came in quick gasps, and sweat gathered between my breasts even though I was still wet from the pool. I unfolded my sunsuit and stepped inside, my hands too shaky to tie the neck straps.

"Oh, but you're covering your lovely suit," he said, slapping his arm on my shoulder.

"Uncle Leon, when did you get here?" I managed to ask, slowly turning toward him.

"Last night. I just came from the concession. Are you heading home?"

"Yes, I was at the pool."

"I can see. I'm going there now. Would you like to use this?"

Leon carried a white towel with the words Shady Grove emblazoned in dark-blue script. He draped the scratchy towel over my shoulders enveloping me. I pulled away, screaming, "No," and flicked it to the ground, repulsed by the thought of him massaging my back and molding the towel down my thighs until he found the spot between my legs.

"Okay, but can you do me a favor?" He reached inside the pocket of his floral Hawaiian shirt. "Can you take this pack of cigarettes to Naomi? She's playing canasta on the porch of our bungalow, the same one we always have by the hill near Ratner's."

"Sure," I said, relieved for a reason to leave Leon. It wasn't even ten, and I had my second delivery job of the day.

When I got to Leon and Naomi's bungalow, there was no one on the porch. The door to the bungalow was open, and I called inside. No answer. I sat on a metal chair for a few minutes, thinking that maybe the women would be here any moment. And then, I heard whistling of the tune "Que Sera, Sera." It was no Doris Day or even James Stewart. It was none other than the utterly disgusting Leon, the lowly reptile. I should have suspected that if Leon and Naomi came the night before, it would have been too soon to arrange for a canasta game in her bungalow. Games were held on the shuffleboard court on such a nice day.

Leon was inside the screened door before I could stand.

"Oh, Mandy. Naomi's game was moved to the lawn." His voice was winded, and sweat beaded his forehead.

"When did you find out?"

"Just now."

Did Leon think that I was born yesterday? Did he think that he could make up any old story and that I would believe every word he said? Did he think he could pretend he hadn't been running to catch me before I left? A man like Leon lived in a world of lies; this one was a little nothing to him.

"Come here," he said, beckoning me to his side.

I stood and tried to wriggle past him, but he blocked the entrance. I turned and ran to the bathroom and slammed the door, fumbling for the lock, a rusty latch hook, and an eyehole. Before I could still my shaking hands to place the hook in the hole, Leon shoved through and pinned me against the sink.

"Mandy," he whispered in my ear, "I've been dreaming of getting close to you again."

"Let me go, Leon. I will scream so the Ratner dogs will come."

Leon slammed his sweaty palm over my lips, and I felt faint. He shoved my neck down so that my face was over his thing, bulging upwards from the side of his matching Hawaiian bathing suit. It was huge and grayish purple and rising like one of my dives. Then he shoved it into my mouth, and I gagged, desperately trying to rotate my head.

"Keep still. It will be over soon," he groaned. "Oh Mandy, push it in, in, inside you deeper."

It was going further in; I wanted to vomit. And then Leon screamed my name again, and my mouth was covered in thick, sticky goop. Leon's thing shrank from my mouth, and I pulled away, gargling and spitting in the sink. He unrolled a wad of toilet paper and wiped himself, his eyes closed and his head rolling. I squirmed from his bulky frame and slunk out the door. I heard Leon yelling, "Don't breathe a word of this, Amanda Gerber, or I'll tell them the truth. You swallowed *me*."

I ran down the porch steps and zoomed through the lawn to Ratner's as if I were competing in an Olympic marathon. When I saw our common driveway, I collapsed on Ratner's front lawn. I couldn't see their dogs, but they must have smelled me or smelled Leon on me because the chorus of yelps got louder. This time, I wanted them to bark and bark and bark.

I sat there while the words to the song Leon whistled played in my head:

When I was just a little girl
I asked my mother, what will I be
Will I be pretty, will I be rich
Here's what she said to me.

Que Sera, Sera,
Whatever will be, will be
The future's not ours, to see
Que Sera, Sera
What will be, will be.

Then Leon's words came back, "You swallowed me." Did I? I tried not to, but I couldn't breathe. Maybe some went down. Even though I hadn't gotten my period yet, I wasn't sure about having a baby. Oh, my God, could I get pregnant from this?

This must have been worse than all those times when Leon took me berry picking, but most of that was a blur of flashes. I had been so young.

What was wrong with me? I could never tell anyone about this, not Laura, not even Francine. By now, I was experienced at keeping secrets inside. Oh no, keep it inside, that's what Leon kept saying.

I had been horrified when my mother admitted the truth about my father's brother Benny, and how he killed himself, how the family kept this a secret for so many years. I had vowed to Nameless, my beloved stuffed animal, that I would never hide from the truth. But I was no better. I was bound genetically to the Gerber clan. I was another liar.

I slumped there on the lawn. The top of my head felt unbearably heavy like I was pinned under a cast-iron frying pan cover. My eyes closed, and I entered that dreamy, drifting state of pre-sleep. My arms locked, straight by my sides; my legs extended like rigid sticks. I felt glued to the grass. Needle tips of light flickered before me in a whirl of seasickness. My head grew larger than my body. Yet, something inside me wasn't scared. Nobody would see what was happening to my body; I was invisible.

·   ·   ·

"M-A-N-D-Y, M-A-N-D-Y! Are you okay?" I heard a female voice through a long tunnel, soft at first, getting louder as the sounds entered my ears.

I couldn't move my mouth. Someone must have cut out my tongue.

"You must have fainted," a voice said.

Through a slit, I recognized Grandma Sarah gliding toward me in slow motion, her feet posed in mid-air like a ballet dancer.

I opened my eyes wider.

"Good, you're coming to. Did you have any breakfast yet?" she asked in an accusing voice. She touched my arm. It felt sharp, hot, and cold. I called upon all my strength.

"I'm okay," I mumbled.

"*Got tsu danken*," thanks to God. My grandmother put an arm under my shoulders to lift me.

"Don't touch me," I said, urgently. "No, I mean, I can get up myself."

·   ·   ·

When we were sitting with my mother at Sarah's kitchen table, with a plate of blintzes and sour cream before me, the women completely convinced that my episode was food-related, I got off the chair and turned toward the door. I needed to get to my place and wash in my own bathtub.

"Did you hear about Leon?" my mother asked my grandmother.

I stopped cold when I heard Leon's name. Did she know?

"What?" Sarah asked.

"He's moving to Florida, with his whole family of course. Leon's brother got him a job in his real estate business."

"Oh, good for them. At least he can recover from the sweater business there."

"Does his brother have children?" I asked.

"Yes, two."

"Are there any girls?"

"No they're boys, why do you ask?"

"No reason, just curious."

I slammed the kitchen door and darted to my cottage, locking the bathroom door behind me. All the while, one single thought stuck in my head: I won't have to see Leon next summer, or maybe ever again. I opened the tap to the bathtub and turned it to the almost-hottest setting. As I flung my sunsuit off, I heard a slight thud. In a bundle of material, still buttressed by the elastic crotch of my sunsuit, laid Naomi's pack of cigarettes, its cellophane glinting in a stream of window light. I opened the pack, shook out the cigarettes over the toilet bowl, pressed the lever, and watched them float away.

THE POWER TO TELL

The mind works in strange ways. The other day, I tried to go back to 1952 and picture the face of my first-grade teacher, Miss Lipschitz. She had a huge, over-sprayed black pompadour, pulled back in a French knot. No matter how much I strained, I couldn't envision the image within her teased frame; but those taunts came rushing back: "Lip shits, lip shits, Miss Lipschitz's lip shits."

I never joined in on those awful singsongs because I knew what it was like to receive them. In my case, the object was my nose, which kept bleeding at the worst possible times, and the person who blurted it to the world was Gerald, my seatmate. He was short and fat and had red-orange hair and lots of tan freckles.

Sometimes, all it took for my nose to bleed was a little wrinkle or two. I always kept a white linen handkerchief on my desk. And Gerald's eyes caught every drop.

"Hey, look who's got a nosebleed today," Gerald would shout, just in case anyone missed it.

Miss Lipschitz kept a black marble composition notebook on her side table, opened to the date. A No. 2 pencil was attached by a green string, hanging between the two sides like a bookmark. When we went to the bathroom, we were supposed to write our names and the times we left and returned.

On one October morning, I sneezed and felt a thick salty wetness ooze into my throat—the signal that my nose was bleeding. I couldn't bear for Gerald to find out. I decided to run to the bathroom, where I could hold my head back until the bleeding stopped. Just before I left, I remembered the notebook. If I bent to sign, I risked the flow of blood. If I didn't, I risked the teacher yelling at me. I scrawled my name and fled, convinced that I had escaped torment.

After I returned to my seat, the teacher inspected the notebook. She looked up and stared straight at me.

"Amanda, did you have another nosebleed?"

Blood must have dripped, after all. "Yes," I whispered.

"Amanda had a nosebleed! Amanda had a nosebleed!" Gerald blared.

My heart pounded so fast, I was sure everyone could hear its drum rolls. Millions of burning prickles radiated from my chest.

That night, like so many others, I couldn't fall asleep. I put my head under the pillow, rehearsing the perfect retort for Gerald. In the morning, I dragged myself out of bed like Hester Prynne on the way to the pillory. All I needed was a scarlet "N" pinned to my blouse. "N" for Nosebleeder.

•　　　•　　　•

Often, my nose bled so hard, I vomited blood. My parents kept towels all over the house; they were scared. My mother took me to have my nose fixed. For me, it wasn't plastic surgery. The doctor placed a pad on my thigh to ground me like a lightning rod, and then stuck a long, silver, electrically heated needle up my nose. My nose was cauterized so often, the hairs in my nostrils forever stood at attention.

Although my nosebleeds eventually became less frequent and stopped in the third grade—could I ever be sure?—Gerald never let me forget them. He was in my second-, third-, fourth-, and fifth-grade classes. Religiously, on the first day of every school year, he'd make the same announcement:

"Don't sit next to Amanda. She gets nosebleeds."

Throughout the year, whenever Gerald spoke to another classmate, and they giggled, I'd assume they were talking about me. I not only tried to avoid Gerald, but I also tiptoed around any boy with a smirk. Not for the first time in my life, I tried to become invisible.

•　　　•　　　•

Sometime between the third and fifth grade, I shamed myself for life. I can't remember the exact year, but it happened in winter, before lunchtime, in the back of the classroom near the coat racks. Five boys, Gerald among them, gathered behind the line of loden coats and fleece-lined jackets. From where I stood, the wool crayon colors moved in and out like flickering Christmas lights.

I went up to my hook, lifted my red plaid coat, and heard a boy's voice from behind.

"Hey, Amanda, is that you?"

"Who's there?"

"It's me, Gerald, and some boys. Come back here."

"What is it?" I asked as I snuck behind the coats.

The boys smiled and looked at me in a funny way, a way I never saw before. My friend Bruce, who shared my birthday, stood on the side of the group. He wore a different look.

"Amanda, come a little closer," Gerald urged.

"What do you want? I'm late for lunch."

"Amanda, if you show us yours, we'll show you ours," Gerald whispered.

"What?"

"You know, your privates." Gerald pointed to his zipper.

"I could never."

"Amanda is a chicken, Amanda is a chicken," Gerald whined.

"I am not!"

"She is, isn't she?" he asked the others.

They all nodded. I looked at Bruce. He turned his head away. Bruce must think me a chicken, too, I thought. And what if Gerald tells the whole school that I have no guts? This, on top of what he says about my nosebleeds.

"Listen, Amanda. You don't have to do a thing. Just, one, two, three, we'll peek, and you can go. And if you want to see ours, you can, too."

I lifted my skirt, slid my pointer finger in the elastic of my underpants, pulled the crotch quickly to the side and back. Then I ran out the room.

That afternoon, I confessed to my mother. I had never told her about the nosebleeds in school or even about Gerald. But this was different. I could be expelled from school. I could be sent to jail.

I couldn't recall what my mother said. It was one of the few times she didn't tell me that when I grew up, I'd have real problems. But I worried anyway. I worried about Gerald and the power he had over me, the power to tell.

•   •   •

Luckily, Gerald was not in my sixth-grade class; I assumed I was in the clear because we would be going to different junior high schools. When I entered my new school, on a cool September morning in 1958, I felt a grown-up sigh of relief. I now knew the truth about noses—and I learned to tiptoe around boys. I also learned to swallow fear and keep it permanently hidden inside my chest.

As I stood in the schoolyard waiting for the whistle to blow, I felt someone tap my shoulder. It was a very short, very fat, and very pimply red-orange-headed boy.

"Gerald!" I shouted.

"Hi, Amanda. I moved over the summer. I guess we're going to the same school."

I wrinkled my nose and clicked my heels together like Dorothy in *The Wizard of Oz*. Maybe I expected to fly home in my magic ruby slippers. Instead, I walked briskly to my classroom, my head high. But once I turned around, I could make out a red-orange blob waving at me.

THE FIGHT

Grandma Sarah burst into my cottage, followed by Laura and Michael. "Amanda, where's your daddy?" my grandmother asked, collapsing on a dining-room chair, her long blue-violet floral skirt hugging her splayed knees.

"Still sleeping," I said. It was not even eight in the morning, and we were, as my mother often said, "not a family that talked before breakfast."

"What is it, Sarah?" my mother asked a lit Chesterfield between her lips. "Are you feeling okay?"

My grandmother sat there breathing hard with her palm pressed to her throat as if she were trying to hold down a popped vein. Her usual pale skin was sweaty and flushed.

"Amanda?" she said.

I was getting scared. She never called me by my full name. I ran to my parents' bedroom and woke my father. Soon, he stood in the living room area, looking confused and alarmed.

"Mother, what is it?" my father asked, his black greasy hair plastered to his skull by sleep and humidity.

"Take Laura and Michael to my room," my mother ordered me, "and close the door."

Laura and I clasped one of three-year-old Michael's hands and swung him down the narrow hallway into my parents' room. I left the door opened a bit but still couldn't make out the conversation.

I asked Laura what was going on. What had riled my grandmother so much that she rushed up the hill from the main country house, which she shared with Laura's family, to our new place?

"Virginia and Sol are fighting real bad," Laura said. When my cousin was upset, she called her parents by their first names. "I think Grandma wanted to get me and my brother out of the house so we wouldn't hear."

After a few minutes, I left Laura and Michael sprawled on my parents' green pile rug, working in Michael's Superman coloring book. On my way to the kitchen to get some bagels, I stopped in the hallway and listened.

"We should call the doctor," my mother said.

"It'll go away," Grandma Sarah said.

"You don't understand. Virginia needs professional help."

"Here goes my wife, Estelle, the amateur psychiatrist," my father said. "I don't want to hear anymore. I'm going to check on the car." I heard the door slam, and the women continued to talk.

"I'll cook a nice chicken," Sarah said. "She'll have a long nap. You'll see, it'll go away."

"But she's making up insane stories. Now it's Bill wanting to have an affair with her. Who knows what's next?"

"Daddy wants to have an affair with Aunt Virginia?" I said, walking into the dining room where the women were sipping coffee. "How could she think that?"

"Mandy, you shouldn't be listening. This is adult talk. Need I remind you that you're still eleven years old?"

"Tell me, I want to know. I have a right to know."

"Oh, you have a right, do you?" My mother slid out another cigarette from the pack in her bathrobe pocket and lit it with the stub of her current cigarette. My father, who always had a cigar in his mouth and shouldn't talk, always said my mother would take a used butt out of the garbage and smoke it if she couldn't find fresh cigarettes.

"Yes, I do," I said, my voice lowering.

"Ok-ay," my mother said, annoyed as if I had been bugging her for hours. "If you must know, it's just Virginia. She thinks from the way your father looked at her last week when we all went to White Lake that he kind of likes her."

"That's crazy. I was sitting right between them on Mr. Siegel's motorboat. He didn't look at her in any special way."

"Okay, okay. Enough, young lady. Don't say a thing to Laura. What are you doing in here anyway?"

"Just getting something to eat for us."

"Get it and hurry back."

The adults stopped talking. I managed to find an excuse to return to the kitchen a few more times. The most I could gather during the next hour or so was that Virginia had calmed and was taking a nap. Grandma Sarah returned to her house and cooked a lot of food. My Uncle Sol took Michael to the village so he could get something for my aunt at the drugstore; Brenda went swimming at the Shady Grove Hotel with the oh-so-handsome lifeguard Bruce Reiger; my mother sat on our terrace, holding a library book in her lap; and my father stretched out on the living-room couch and listened to the Dodgers on the radio. It seemed like any other Catskill summer day in 1957.

•   •   •

Our fathers, like the other men from the neighboring bungalow colonies, drove back to the city, or in some cases, the suburbs, after dinner on Sunday evenings, leaving their wives and other female relatives to supervise the children. When our fathers were getting ready to leave, I heard a lot of whispering by the cars. My mother whispered to my father, and then to my uncle. Grandma Sarah whispered to her two sons, and then Sol whispered something to Laura. Everything seemed quiet, quiet as a whisper.

The kitchen screen door swung open, and Aunt Virginia emerged. She had a one-sided teased beehive and unblotted rouge cheek circles and was holding a screaming and squirming Michael. She walked toward her car. "Solly, Solly," she yelled in a voice that sounded like a little girl whimpering in the dark. "Solly, you can't go."

"You know I have to. I can't ignore my job."

"Let Bill handle it."

"I can't, Ginny. You know Bill and I are not in the same business anymore. You'll be fine."

My aunt's complaints turned into sobs.

"Calm down, Ginny. How can Bill and I go back to the city if you're like this?"

"*Now* what's wrong with her?" my mother shrieked. Despite my mother's reading of the latest psychology books, she wasn't patient with crazy behavior. Her small brown eyes were puffy from lack of sleep, and her brown hair drooped from the curled split ends of an old permanent.

"Nothing, nothing," Sol said, holding his sides. "I gotta run to the toilet."

"There must be curses in the air today," my grandmother said. "Maybe it's something we ate."

Speaking of food, Grandma Sarah handed my father bags filled with it so her sons shouldn't starve during the week. Sol returned to his car, and Laura hugged and kissed him good-bye; I gave my father a peck on the cheek, and we stood with the rest of the family around the cars. Aunt Virginia, yelling, "Wait a second," ran back in the house to get her own package of food for Sol. The minute Virginia was out of sight, my mother said to Sol, "Don't worry about a thing. We'll take care of her."

Our fathers drove off, and I sat on the grass by the Sun House gazebo instead of running down the driveway with Laura, who waved wildly until her father's car was a blur.

•   •   •

On Wednesday right before dinner, Brenda entered the Sun House where Laura and I were playing our 102nd game of war, this time with two decks.

"They're at it again," Brenda said. "I just couldn't take them anymore."

"What are you talking about?" I asked.

"I was in the main house with Grandma Sarah. We were in her room so she could fix my blouse on the sewing machine. I could hear our mothers fighting."

"About what?" Laura asked.

"I think your mother was about to call your father in the city, and my mother was trying to talk her out of it."

"Why?"

"You got me," Brenda said and shrugged.

Our mothers must have gone into the kitchen because now we could hear them screaming.

"If I want to call him, I'll call him! You can't stop me," my aunt shouted.

"You'll just make him worry for nothing."

"But I want to tell him."

"Tell him what, about another man?"

"He should know that Harvey made a pass at me. Now that Solly's got a *shiksa* at the hardware store, why shouldn't he know about Harvey?"

"There's no *shiksa,* and there's nothing to tell Sol. You're the one who called Harvey and begged him to take you out someplace. Just leave the phone alone. The men will be here in just two days."

"There is another woman I tell you."

"How in the world do you know, Virginia?"

"When I was in the village last weekend, I saw Isidore outside the gas station and asked him if he'd seen Sol. He pointed to the hardware store. I went there and watched them from the window. They were talking in a cozy way."

"That's hardly proof," my mother said.

The women probably returned to the hallway phone because we couldn't distinguish any more conversation, just a lot of yelling and slamming.

"I wonder what's going on," Laura said.

My fifteen-year-old sister sat quietly. She unsnapped her gold butterfly barrette and regathered her thick shoulder-length hair to re-pin it. Looking at Laura, she said, "Oh, it's probably nothing. You know how our mothers are. Neither of them is exactly Minnie Mouse."

"I guess," Laura said, unconvincingly.

A few minutes later, my mother slipped out the door and called us home for dinner.

That was the last time that week I heard the women fight. Everything seemed peaceful, with Virginia spending a lot of time in her room or outside in her nightgown lying in the lounge chair between our two houses. The only company we had was the neighbor's handyman Lester who came to speak to my mother about something—possibly a chore or two.

•　　•　　•

On Friday night when the men drove up in their cars, the kitchen door of the main house opened, and a brand-new Virginia slunk out. Her wavy auburn hair flowed straight down, brushed shiny. A red hairband held a pink Kleenex carnation with a green pipe-cleaner stem that Laura and I made that afternoon at Siegel's Bungalow Colony, where we had started a twice-weekly day camp with the five- and six-year-olds. Virginia wore blue-cuffed shorts, a yellow strapless tube top, sandals with cork heels, and hot-pink lipstick. She looked very glamorous.

My uncle whistled, and my aunt's smile broadened; then my father whistled, and Virginia froze, and smoke seemed to come out of her nostrils. My mother and I were standing on the porch of our house and could see it all. My mother let out a whoosh as if she were exhaling a large drag of her cigarette, and went inside, slamming the screen door. I ran down the stairs and dashed to my father's car, taking a pillowcase stuffed with his laundry from the trunk. I followed him into our house; my uncle, his arm around his wife, walked toward his.

•　　•　　•

Laura and I didn't see each other until the next morning when I tapped the screen window in Grandma Sarah's room under the apple trees. Luckily, Laura, who slept in the second twin bed, formerly Brenda's, was up and my grandmother's chest was heaving, a sure sign that she was snoring. I motioned for my cousin to unhook the screen and crawl out. Soon we were giggling in the Sun House, making plans for the day.

We spent the rest of the morning at the Big Rock in the woods behind my house, talking, reading comics, taking a break and tanning on the Sun Rock with aluminum foil under our chins, and then going back to the Big Rock to cool off. I dozed for a minute and dreamed I was swimming in the pool at Siegel's.

"I guess we should go back soon," Laura said when we got hungry. "My mother's going to kill me if we're not there for lunch."

"I guess," I said. "Laura?"

"What?"

"Let's make a pledge." I remembered two years ago when Laura and I had merged our bloodied fingers together, pressing lifetime allegiance.

"What?"

"Let's swear by blood cousins that whatever happens to us, we'll always come back to our secret rock."

"Nothing's going to happen."

"I know, but let's do it anyway, for extra protection."

"Okay."

"And, Laura, promise you'll never come to our rock with anyone but me."

"Who else would I come with?"

"Promise?"

"Okay, I promise."

"I promise too that I won't either."

I scrunched, dug into our hiding place and pulled out two old arrows from under the pile of leaves, then climbed back up the Big Rock. Standing, I held up the arrows, crossed them together back and forth like swords before a duel, and said in a very official-sounding voice: "We swear by blood cousins that this is our rock and we'll never take anyone else here, no matter what."

Laura repeated the pledge after I told her that we didn't have to do anything with blood, and we lay on our rock afterward, not talking, trying to swat the leaves on the tree with our arrow sticks.

We swept pebbles and dried mud off our rock with twigs and jumped off and took a good look from a few feet away. For the first time, I noticed that our rock was shaped like a whale and that the oak tree behind it looked like it was a tall spout. I didn't know about Laura, but at that moment, I felt warm and liquidy inside, as I imagined a young married couple would feel standing in front of their very first house. With my arm slipped under Laura's, I said, "Well, blood cousin, there she is, our rock, a whale of a rock, the finest rock in the world."

•　　•　　•

It turned out that Laura didn't have to worry about being away too long. There was so much noise and silence when we got back that nobody would have paid attention even if King Kong swooped down and scooped up Laura and me in his big furry hands.

Before we had reached the wishing well behind my house, I heard our neighbor's dogs barking continuously, but there were no sounds of cars driving up or down our driveway. Past my house, I could see my uncle's turquoise-and-white Oldsmobile near the Sun House, the trunk lid open.

"What do you think is going on?" I asked Laura.

"I don't know."

We reached the apple trees and sat between them. Soon, we saw Virginia racing to the car carrying bulging shopping bags. Sol was rushing behind her, trying to stop her with his arm. "Ginny, slow down," he said.

"You can't change my mind," she said.

"But the children?"

"I'm not staying here a minute longer, and neither are they."

"Where do you want to go?"

"Back home to the city, our real home."

"You're leaving!" I gasped to Laura.

"Oh no!" she said. "But it can't be. It's not time yet, the summer isn't over. There are two weeks left." Laura started to cry.

My aunt's voice got louder. "You just don't understand. Bill is in love with me, and Lester tried to murder Michael. Estelle paid him."

"You're talking nonsense," my uncle said.

"Am I? Well, even Doctor Sugarman says it's possible."

"Lester and my mother tried to murder your brother?" I repeated to Laura in a flat voice like a robot.

"We must have heard wrong," Laura said.

"All I know," I said, "is that my mother told me that she offered Lester money to kill the weeds by the wishing well."

We listened for a few more minutes, but the adults no longer said anything. My aunt shoved the bags in the trunk; Laura and I clutched each other's shaking hands. As my aunt turned and headed for the house, she saw us sitting by the apple trees. "What are you girls doing there? Are you spying?"

"No, Mommy," Laura said, her voice trembling with tears. "We were just resting here."

"Get in the house now! And get away from that girl."

"From Mandy?"

"You heard me, MOVE!"

Laura ran inside, and I dashed to my house, flopped on the living-room couch, and pressed my face to the window, my eyes glued to Laura's car, willing her not to get inside. I wanted to run and grab her, blast the car horn to divert the adults' attention, and lead Laura back to our rock. But I couldn't move my arms or legs; I was aware of a fist-throbbing in my chest and a screw-tightening of my forehead. I didn't understand what was happening to me, but felt I would never recover.

My mother and my grandmother were talking loudly in my parents' room.

"*Oy vay iz mir*—what will happen to her?" Grandma Sarah said.

"I wish I knew."

"Doctor Sugarman said she just needs a rest," my grandmother said.

"She's paranoid. She's very sick," my mother said and then their voices lowered, and I couldn't understand the rest. I didn't know what paranoid was, but I knew it was bad.

Maybe ten minutes later, Laura and her family got into the car, drove down the driveway, and headed in the direction of the village, the first landmark on the long drive to the city. A giant "NO" was enlarging rapidly in my mouth, blocking my vocal cords. The Ratner dogs yelped for another five minutes, and then there was no barking, no noise, nothing. Even my mother and grandmother broke up their conversation and left the house without speaking a word.

• • •

That night I couldn't fall asleep. I kept replaying the adult conversations, searching for a clue that they didn't happen as I remembered. As soon as I closed my eyes, I saw Laura's blotchy, tear-streaked, downturned face, unable to point directly at me.

I must have fallen asleep eventually because when I opened my eyes, it was light out and I went to the bathroom to pee. Without changing from my pajamas, I tiptoed out of the house and found myself in front of Laura's window. I peeked inside in the hope that her family drove up during that sliver of time I was sleeping, and she'd be in her bed. But it was empty.

In a kind of trance, I set off towards the woods. Suddenly I was in front of the Big Rock. I admired its curved shape and how the oak tree formed a perfect umbrella over its gray surface. I smoothed my hands over the rock in a circular motion as if clearing a path. Then I bent and kissed it, repeating my words to Laura the day before when we were last here together: "Well, blood cousin, there she is, our rock, a whale of a rock, the finest rock in the world."

TUTTI FRUTTI FOR ME

I was watching *The Adventures of Ozzie and Harriet* on the giant Admiral 21-inch console television, and I couldn't wait for the commercial to raid the freezer and see if there was any ice cream. My father, mother, and sister were in the living room; but it was no use asking them because my father would not have answered, my sister would have ordered me to bring her a bowl of whatever I found, and my mother would have said that I should look myself if I wanted anything that badly. Besides, what I was longing for did not exist in this small Brooklyn apartment. I needed tutti frutti ice cream, and the flavors my mother bought were butter pecan for my father and chocolate for my sister. Every time I told my mother that I didn't have the same taste as my sister, she seemed surprised and said, "Why, I thought chocolate was your favorite." I always answered her with the truth, "I love vanilla." But I might as well have said tutti frutti because she never listened to me.

The reason I was crazy with the tutti frutti was because in the show, the Nelsons see a story in the newspaper about a police sergeant who is keeping a lost boy happy with a large tutti frutti cone, entertaining him until his parents show up. This is the one night the Nelsons decide to forgo dessert to cut down on calories. Ricky, the troublemaker, wants tutti frutti badly. Darning socks, wearing a high-necked sweater with a double strand of pearls, Harriet Nelson says, "I haven't tasted tutti frutti in years."

Ozzie and Harriet reminisce about their youth and where they bought large portions of this flavor. "Somehow you just don't get ice cream like that anymore," Ozzie says, and David follows, "You don't get anything like that anymore." Clearly, the Nelsons, dubbed by the announcer as, "America's Favorite Family" who enjoy "good times together," also agree about this lack of uniqueness in modern culture.

• • • •

Even though it was a cold night in December 1957, my mouth watered, and I raced to the kitchen. The freezer was crammed with a tundra of yellowing ice. A carton of Birds Eye frozen peas peeked out between the craters like the first spring growth in an arctic melt; and clinging to the side, pinned against the freezer edge, was a one-pint box of pistachio ice cream, my father's second favorite. I opened the carton, and there were maybe two spoonfuls caked in frost. Not bothering to get a Pyrex bowl, I took the container and a spoon back to the living room and watched Ozzie, who is now in bed, immersed in a dream.

"You could have brought me some," Brenda, said.

"I didn't want to miss the show," I said.

"Only an animal eats from the carton."

I growled, pounced, and swung my arms wildly. I pulled each of my brown braids straight from my ears and opened my mouth in a huge circle, my small brown eyes like dots of surprise.

"Mother, your younger daughter is a monkey and belongs in the zoo."

"Yeah, she's as dumb as an ape," my father said, looking up from the *New York Post*'s sports page. He sat at the far end of the small rectangular living room in his threadbare, red scotch-plaid captain's chair, his slippered feet splayed on the matching ottoman. This was the first thing he had said all evening.

In Ozzie's dream, he and Harriet are sitting in an old-fashioned ice-cream parlor. It takes place in their youth, maybe in the 1920s. Harriet wears a cloche hat with a feather and a flapper dress; Ozzie sports a bow tie and striped blazer. Then, Harriet bursts out singing "Goody Goody" in a throaty voice, as if she has smoked a pack of Chesterfields. Backing her up is the singing group, the Four Preps, echoing "goody goody for him" and "goody goody for me."

Before long, Ricky is singing, "You got it comin' to ya," and the audience belts out, "Hooray and hallelujah." The refrain "goody goody" becomes "tutti frutti," with Ozzie and Harriet, followed by the Four Preps, singing, "Tutti frutti for me." If that's not enough, Harriet and other women do the Charleston. Harriet pumps her arms and kicks her legs and moves into a solo while Ozzie accompanies with his banjo.

And that was why I loved Harriet above all the other TV moms. She was not Margaret Anderson making dinner and kissing her husband when he gets home from his important job at the insurance company, convinced that father knows best. She was not Mrs. Goldberg yoo-hooing out her window while awaiting her family's arrival. She was not Alice Kramden mocking her wacky husband as he schemes away her poverty. Beneath Harriet's short, modest bob and no-nonsense clothes, she was her own woman, even in Ozzie's dreams.

•　　•　　•

I whipped my spoon around the bottom of the pistachio container because I liked it best when it had a creamy consistency, and I scraped the bottom. Finally, I plunged in my pointer finger, wiping it along the edges, licking it for the final taste.

"Stop making those annoying noises!" Brenda said. "I can't hear the show."

The front door slammed; and because Brenda, my mother, and I were still in the living room, I knew my father had gone out, and he wasn't looking for ice cream. My mother's shoulders popped up, and she turned her head toward the hallway and then resumed reading her book. She was a big-time reader, taking out at least one book a week at the library. Her favorite subject was British royalty, and she knew every king and queen in succession, plus their offspring. All I knew was that Henry VIII was ugly and wore a funny collar that looked like my crinoline squashed into a beehive.

"You girls better stay off the phone tonight," my mother said.

I didn't question her because I didn't want her to realize that it was after 9 p.m. on a Wednesday, and most mothers would say it was too late to be on the phone on a school night. Not that my mother was like most mothers. With her unblemished complexion, dimpled nose tip, and thick upswept chestnut hair, she was prettier than Harriet Nelson and even Loretta Young. Not that prettiness ever helped her. It was both good and bad that, when it came to being like other mothers, she left me alone.

My mother probably didn't remember, too, that Wednesday night at nine was the absolute cutoff for Brenda to receive calls for a Saturday night date. Brenda wouldn't pick up the phone if I gave her an Elvis record. She would rather parade around on a Saturday afternoon on Flatbush Avenue, her long legs sticking out from her tight black pencil skirt and with her hair in rollers (not that she needed them since she gave herself a smelly Toni home permanent) under a scarf, and pretend she was having a date that night rather than accept an offer on Wednesday at 9:15. Just turning sixteen, Brenda was an expert on the teen rules for dating.

I didn't want to remind my mother about phone etiquette because I knew what she was thinking, and it wasn't good. Last Friday night, I was on the phone with Francine, and then Brenda was on the phone with a boy for at least an hour, when my father came home after the news stinking of whiskey.

Proudly, he said, "I was in jail."

My mother for once was silent.

Brenda said, "You're kidding, Daddy?"

"No, there I was with the boys at Angelo's playing poker, and we got busted by two cops for gambling. Can you believe it? They even took my shoelaces."

"Why?" I asked, more startled at this than the fact that my father was in jail.

"So he wouldn't hang himself, stupid," Brenda said.

"Bill, why didn't you call and tell us where you were? We were getting worried."

Of course, I didn't correct my mother then. I didn't think anyone noticed that he wasn't home since he had been either sitting in his chair all day not talking, still wearing his soiled striped pajamas, or sleeping in the bedroom for huge chunks of time, my family accustomed to his absence. My father had been lucky that night. He'd explained that the judge laughed and let them go.

"Did you get your shoelaces back?" I asked.

My father went into the bathroom without answering. All I could hear was the long, steady stream of his pee, which I had to wipe from the toilet seat that he once again forgot to lift.

•   •   •

I placed the empty ice-cream carton on the coffee table and covered my lap with an old afghan, pulling it up toward my mouth so I could bite my nails without Brenda noticing.

After the Charleston, Ozzie wants to charge the two ice creams, but Dave, who acts as the waiter, won't allow him. Before Ozzie and Harriet can taste them, Dave takes away the two multi-scooped ice-cream tulip sundae glasses from the table. In a semi-sleep, Ozzie pleads, "David, come back and give me my tutti frutti."

I couldn't say why this made me cry. I couldn't take Ozzie's frustration. I wanted him to have his ice cream already.

At this point, Brenda forgot that she just ordered me to shut up and started to hum, "Tutti Frutti au rutti, a-bop-bop-a-loom-op, a-lop bop boom!"

"Shh," I whispered.

"Brenda, please," my mother said, one of the rare times she seemed to be on my side.

"Oh Mother, that was a Little Richard song," Brenda said. "You know the guy who was in that Alan Freed movie. You've heard him on the radio lots of times."

"You think I know Little Richard from Big Daddy?"

"No, but you know Richard III," I said, swearing I could see an upturned crease in my mother's penciled cat's eyes.

Poor Ozzie is now a crazed man and goes to his neighbor Darby in the middle of the night, begging him to look in his freezer for tutti frutti. No luck. Later, Harriet and Ozzie get dressed to go out and search for tutti frutti.

• • • •

There was a commercial. In the beginning of the show, Ozzie introduced the Kodacolor 135 film, the "biggest 35 mm news since color slides." This time, it's not Ozzie, but another man, and he presents "one of the world's great cameras," a Kodak Retina Reflex, for the professional and advanced amateur. But these people at Kodak are smart. They know their audience. The man now takes out the Pony II, for those people just getting started in color slides. He says it's amazingly simple to use and only costs $26.75, adding the kicker: The Nelson family found it a real pleasure to use.

I wanted to punch the television screen and wipe off his royal smugness. Of course, the Nelsons could afford any camera they wanted and could probably get a Kodak for nothing. Who were they fooling? The only thing the Nelsons couldn't get was tutti frutti ice cream.

This Pony still looked very fancy, and I wished I could have a camera even if it was a Brownie. But since my father lost his sweater business over a year ago, partly from investing in a new sideline of taffeta cocktail dresses, I was lucky to still get money for an occasional Archie comic.

Ozzie and Harriet find a drugstore with a light on, and the druggist searches his freezer. The closest he can come to tutti frutti is cherry. When they return home, the whole family is awake and gathers at the kitchen table. Ever resourceful, Harriet serves them fruit cocktail to mix with the cherry ice cream, her approximation of tutti frutti.

• • •

I remembered when I made ice cream with Francine three years ago when I was nine. In her kitchen on East 22nd Street in Flatbush, two buildings from mine on the dead end, I helped Francine search her mother's cookbooks for an ice-cream recipe. I was impressed that Francine's mother, Mrs. Nederlander, had a cookbook with food stains on the red-and-white checkered cover. As far as I knew, my mother never consulted a recipe, though she once read an article that said it was healthy to have two different colored vegetables for dinner, and the one thing she could think of besides green was yellow. So, every other night, Brenda and I ate wax beans. At least, this got my father to say something funny, a rhyme that for a long while I thought he'd made up: "Beans, beans, the musical fruit. The more you eat, the more you toot."

Anyhow, Mrs. Nederlander's cookbook contained a recipe for ice cream, and it was for vanilla, my favorite. Francine and I got out a carton of eggs from the refrigerator and had no trouble assembling the other ingredients. Then the recipe called for separating the eggs and setting aside the egg whites, and we were stuck. "What does separate mean?" Francine had asked.

Being a year older, I was too embarrassed to admit that I didn't know. "Put them in separate rooms," I said, hoping the joke would cover my ignorance. Then I got a brainstorm, "It must mean that you make hard-boiled eggs and then you can get whites and yellows."

Without missing a beat, Francine got out the biggest pot in the cabinet, and we boiled the eggs until most cracked. Gently, with a large spoon, I lifted each out of the boiling water and, when they cooled to the touch, Francine and I peeled the shells, pried open the eggs, scooped out the yellows, and deposited the egg-white chunks into Mrs. Nederlander's brand-new, red, electric mixing bowl. I may not remember that I didn't know what "fold" meant and left that chore to Francine, but I'll never forget the entrance of the Nederlanders.

"P-yew, what is that odor?" Mr. Nederlander had asked, pinching his nostrils together.

"Are you girls cooking something?" Mrs. Nederlander asked, looking toward the kitchen as if she were expecting the Fire Department with hoses drawn.

"It's like a sulfur factory in here," Mr. Nederlander said.

But unlike my father, who would not have missed an opportunity to point out that my friend and I were dimwits, and unlike my mother, who would have shrieked louder than she did when she came home every night from her new job as a bookkeeper, and I didn't clean the house to her satisfaction, Mr. Nederlander opened the kitchen window and his wife dusted hard-boiled egg bits from her cookbook. Afterward, I heard them laughing hysterically in the den they used for a television room. In a cage hanging from a hook near the window facing the courtyard, Francine's parrot, Timothy, screeched, "happy happy," and I left Francine's yearning for a bird who talked, among other things.

•   •   •

Ozzie calls the police officer, Sergeant Dolan, from the newspaper and asks him where he bought the tutti frutti he gave to the lost boy.

Brenda stretched and said, "Enough with the tutti frutti! I still can't believe that Jerry Lee Lewis got married today."

"Yeah, I heard," I said. "It was his cousin."

"It's unbelievable. She is only a year older than you."

"What's that?" my mother asked, her voice louder than her usual loudness.

"She was only thirteen," I said.

"Who is?" my mother said.

Just then the phone rings. Brenda and I exchanged raised eyebrows. My father hadn't been out long enough for him to be locked up in jail again.

"I'll get it," my mother said, with a tone of annoyance. Even she realized it couldn't be my father.

"Oh, no," I heard my mother say from the hallway where the black rotary sat on the mahogany secretary.

"When did it happen?" she said in a voice rushed with worry. "Of course."

After a few more words that I couldn't make out, my mother stood in the living room entranceway, her rosy cheeks blanched.

"What?" Brenda and I said simultaneously.

"I have some terrible news," my mother said.

"Was Daddy in an accident?" I asked.

"No . . . it's my sister," she said in a barely audible voice, followed by an "oh-h-h," and a choking, crying sound.

Aside from a loud fight with my grandmother Mashie last summer, I had never seen my mother cry. Terrified, I said, "Aunt Louise?"

"Yes," my mother mumbled. "She just died. Nadine will come here to stay with us while her father takes care of things."

My heart sank and then exploded in my chest. It felt like I swallowed the whole thing, swiveling up my windpipe and beating in my mouth. My aunt was forty-two, two years older than my mother. Their brother Barry had been killed in World War II; Brenda was named after him. My mother's other sister Rebecca had mental problems, though nobody talked about her except to say that she used to be a beauty. Aunt Louise was fine until six months ago, and then she had some bad headaches and acted strangely and now she was dead from a brain tumor. I wondered if this was inherited. I wondered if my mother's family was doomed.

No matter how much my mother and father acted strangely, I couldn't imagine them ever dying. If my mother ever got seriously sick, I expected her to fall and bang her fists on the linoleum floor in the kitchen, refusing to give in to fate. I remembered seeing *The Eddy Duchin Story* and how I cried when Tyrone Power, playing Eddy, died of leukemia at forty and that was a real-life story. When my mother did her *New York Times* crossword puzzle on Sundays, she played the movie music on the Victrola, something by Chopin. She claimed that Chopin was schmaltzier than Beethoven, but that didn't stop her from playing the record so many times, there were permanent skips in three places.

"Amanda," my mother said as she pivoted toward her bedroom. "Being the same age, it's up to you to be extra nice to Nadine. Remember when your aunt was first diagnosed, how much she counted on you to spend time with Nadine."

My mother slipped into her room and closed the door. Brenda turned down the volume on the television.

"Oh my God," she said. "I can't believe Aunt Louise is dead. Poor Nadine."

"I know," I said, remembering one girl in my class, Rhoda, whose father died from a heart attack. Everyone in the class talked about it and looked at Rhoda as if she had leprosy.

I listened at my mother's door. There were no sobbing noises. I heard what sounded like furniture squeaking, and then my mother yelling my name and saying, "If that is you spying by the door, please go away and leave me alone. Finish watching your show."

Brenda turned up the volume, and we both sat on the sofa transfixed.

I had missed what seemed like Ozzie and Darby getting lost following Sergeant Dolan's directions. Finally, they find a drugstore that has tutti frutti. In the next scene, they delight in their piled-high ice-cream cones with none other than Sergeant Dolan. Ozzie calls Harriet and says, "Why don't you and the boys get lost and come down here."

But I couldn't concentrate on Ozzie and Darby. I kept thinking that any second now, my cousin Nadine will be here. What will I say to her? How will she behave? I knew this was terribly selfish, but I couldn't stop thinking about Nadine moving into my room and sharing my bed. Not that I minded the squishing together, but it was Nadine that bothered me. She thought she was a big shot because she had a television and a piano in her bedroom, and she wouldn't let me touch either one. I once heard my mother say, "Louise and Jack spoil Nadine as if this can make up for their absences."

Nadine also bragged about Jerry Feinstein in my class. She called him her boyfriend because he once came to her house and they watched *I Love Lucy* on her tiny television, and he kissed her. But I knew for a fact that he called Francine and asked her to go to a party, and Mrs. Nederlander said she was too young to go on a date without a chaperone.

"Ugh," Brenda said.

"What?"

"All that ice cream in the middle of the night."

I admitted that Ozzie and Darby's tutti frutti ice cream looked disgusting. It reminded me of that icky fruitcake people ate at Christmas. By now, I felt a little nauseous. I was happy that Ozzie and Darby got what they craved. I was happy that the whole Nelson family joined in the search and accompanied Ozzie in both reality and in his dreams.

And while I realized that this Nelson family was not real, that Ozzie never seemed to have a job, that Harriet never acted annoyed, that Ricky got the attention, and that Dave, though pretty cute, always suffered from his brother's talent, still they were really the Nelsons. They weren't what they seemed, but they were America's Favorite Family, enjoying good times together.

• • •

The doorbell rang, and I caught my breath, startled. I knew it wasn't my father because he would use his key. My mother came out of her room, her full lips freshly painted with Hazel Bishop's no-smear secret red, holding a lit Chesterfield with the ash almost as long as the tip.

"I'll get it," she muttered, the same thing she said when she picked up the phone minutes ago.

My mother opened the door, and Cousin Nadine stood there with her cleaning lady Gladys.

"Darling," my mother said, clutching Nadine to her chest. "This is so, so terrible."

Nadine broke away from my mother's grip. She unbuttoned her camel car coat, threw it on my father's empty chair, and lumbered to the sofa. "Make room," she said to me, shoving me to the side. "Did I miss Ricky and David?"

It was the end of the episode and Ozzie announces a new Kodak Signet 50 camera with flash, only $82.50.

"I'm going to get that," Nadine said.

Now was not the time to remind Nadine that her father had a brand-new 8 mm movie camera. I watched the credits and heard the announcer say that Ozzie and Harriet are brought to you on film from Eastman Kodak Company . . . "your guarantee of quality."

GRANDMA SARAH'S FUNERAL

I didn't see Laura for almost a year and a half, not until I was thirteen, not until Grandma Sarah's funeral. On a below-zero January morning in 1959, my relatives gathered at Futterman's Funeral Home in Sheepshead Bay, and greeted us, the immediate family, in a small waiting room outside the chapel. My mother, my sister Brenda, and I sat on a green leather couch, flanked by end tables. From a hole in the center of each table, a brass-necked lamp sprung out like a miniature umbrella, its dim orange light falling on a blue crocheted-covered tissue box and a tiny seashell ashtray stacked with Futterman's business cards.

My father and Uncle Sol were in another room, talking to the rabbi; and as we waited for them, all I could do was stare at the room's entrance. Every time I saw a shape flutter behind clustering groups by the doorway, I expected to see my cousins—Laura, now twelve, and her brother, Michael, going on five—and, of course, my aunt who would be stunning in black.

Since she had a terrible fight with my mother, Virginia had forbidden her children to see my family. I pleaded with my parents to arrange something—a sneak meeting at Grandma Sarah's . . . an overlapping appointment at the dentist's . . . attached dryers at the beauty parlor. My mother worked on my father, and my father worked on Uncle Sol, but nobody could budge Virginia, and everyone was afraid to try too hard. A few times I called Laura's house and hung up when Virginia answered.

For the seventeen long months that Laura and I were separated, I became a nut case picturing what the other Gerbers would look like. Would Laura still be chubby, with swaying pigtails, and have that awkward, draggy walk? Would Michael still be the cute little blond boy? And would my aunt slink in the room like a movie star; or would she twitter and shake, showing the lines and darting eyes of a woman, who, by now I had heard often enough, was just "not well"?

Many nights I'd lie in my bed, imagining possible Lauras. Sometimes she'd be slow-motion waving at me, her heart-shaped mouth frozen in a silent sob, like she did when I last saw her drive away from our country houses in Mountainview. Sometimes she'd have red-tracked cheeks like she did after we pricked our fingers and pressed them together as blood cousins; sometimes she'd be growing out of control like Jack's gigantic beanstalk, and I'd be powerless to reach her. Mostly, I'd stretch her into a longer version of my memory, and we'd still be a similar height and weight. Once I got out of bed and took my scrapbook, scissors, crayons, and a bottle of glue to the bathroom; closed the door; turned on the light; and went to work. I took Laura's ten-year-old face, trimmed off her pigtails, added some midriff with a flesh Crayola crayon, pasted a skirt over her chewed-up bare legs, and taped this Laura to the bathroom mirror, to see if she resembled herself— or, with her tangled hair finally straightened and her unibrow divided, if she looked more like me.

And on so many, so many afternoons, I'd take detours after school on my way home. I'd turn on Ocean Avenue, Laura's street, and stop a few blocks from her building, pretending to tie my shoe or pick up a book, hoping and praying she'd happen to walk by. It got so bad that I'd expect to see her almost anywhere, even places she'd never been to, like my doctor, my ballet school, my supermarket.

One Saturday morning, when I was twelve, Francine and I went to Macy's on Flatbush Avenue. We were giggling in the dressing room when we heard what sounded like a mother and daughter fighting in the next booth. The woman said, "Just try it on for God's sake." The girl said, "I told you a thousand times, I hate it." Then the woman shouted at the top of her lungs, "You hate everything! Go naked for all I care. You're giving me a conniption fit." I had never heard anyone else say that. It had to be them.

I froze. Francine asked me what was wrong. Dropping the jacket I was about to try on, I motioned her to be quiet. I put my ear against the adjoining wall and listened, but there were no sounds. Maybe they took a yelling break; all I could hear was a lot of clacking like someone throwing plastic hangers on the floor. I went to the curtain and drew it enough to peek out, and waited. Finally, a woman and a girl my age walked out. The mother had clothes strewn over her arm. I caught a glimpse of their fronts. Even though I wasn't sure how Laura looked, I saw enough of the girl's face to know it wasn't her.

Fifteen minutes before Grandma Sarah's funeral, I recalled all those times I wondered about Laura—what she did during July when her family went to the country, and we stayed in the city . . . whether she helped Grandma Sarah pinch the corners of her doughy *kreplach* meat dumplings . . . where she went in August when Mountainview became mine again. Most of all, I wondered if Laura thought as much about me, if she longed to see me like I longed to see her, if she also felt a part of her was missing. I thought of all this, sitting on that green leather couch, waiting for my father and uncle to agree on what to say about their dead mother.

Everyone quieted while those standing near the door moved away as if they just remembered they were at a funeral. It was my Grandma Sarah's sister, my great-aunt Olga, with my Uncle Isidore. Olga wore a black wool dress and a black pillbox hat with a black-netted veil.

"Close your mouth!" Brenda whispered to me.

"It's amazing. I've never seen them so dressed up."

"I know," Brenda said.

"I've never seen them outside Mountainview, outside their candy store, except for a few times at our house in the country. It's funny to see them here."

We stood to kiss them when a man from the funeral parlor told us it was time to go into the chapel. My heart thumped wildly. I thought I would never get my feet to move. I looked at my Aunt Olga. The veil on her face had little black velvet decorations. The way they hung on her nose, they looked like snotballs. As we walked down the aisle toward the front row, I felt everyone looking at me. I imagined Olga's nose and felt whoops of laughter collecting in my throat. Oh, no, I thought. I'd better swallow hard. I just can't laugh. Not now. Not here.

My mother, Brenda, and I sat on the stiff, wooden pew in the front row. From there, I could see my grandmother's coffin, perched on a platform below the stage. My mother had asked Brenda and me if we wanted to see my grandmother in the viewing room. We both said "no" like we had it rehearsed. Even though the casket was now closed, I still didn't want to look straight ahead, so I kept turning around, watching people pass, watching them look from side to side as if trying to find seats at a wedding ceremony.

My father and Uncle Sol were next. I had seen my uncle twice since the summer that Laura left; but, now, walking alongside my father, he looked like *he* was the older brother. Overnight, it seemed to me, he turned gray on his sideburns; the back of his head was still black. He walked with a stoop, not in the bouncy, dancing way that I remembered. But it was hard to know if the changes were permanent; after all, I kept telling myself, both men were at their mother's funeral.

When they got to the front, the men separated. My father turned right and sat next to me; Sol went to the left row, which was empty except for a black bible and a black yarmulke. Then I heard several voices going "shh." If we had been at a wedding, this would be the time for the bride to march down the aisle. But it was my Aunt Virginia, as pretty as I knew she'd be, with her hair pulled back in a French knot, walking slowly in a black crepe dress; followed by a slim-figured young woman, a copy of my aunt; followed by Michael, skipping, trying to catch up with his mother and sister. Laura was even more beautiful than I had imagined when I cut her up into tiny pieces and glued her together in my scrapbook.

As Laura reached her father, she stood still, tilted her head to the right, and glanced up and down my row. Just as the rabbi came out a side door onto the stage and walked to the lectern, above my grandmother's coffin, Laura's eyes met mine. We smiled shyly. Then she turned around and said something to my aunt Olga who was sitting in the row behind her.

Laura looked in my direction. I wondered if she had noticed the way the veil fell over Olga's face. She seemed to wink at me, and I felt those heaving, laughing waves fill my throat again, pushing to get out. I held my hand over my mouth and started making little cough-like sounds to hide escaping gasps. I was hoping people would think I was choking, not laughing. I didn't risk looking at Laura again because I was so close to losing what little control I had; all I needed was another sign from her, and I'd be a goner.

Something was definitely wrong with me. It was bad enough that I couldn't cry, no matter how much I tried by thinking of past sad things like when my mother's brother was killed in the war or when my aunt Louise died last year. But nothing worked. All I could do was sit there and hope I wouldn't laugh out loud.

I breathed in and out, trying to concentrate on the rabbi. I couldn't really follow the religious stuff; but whenever he mentioned my grandmother, I wondered: Who is he talking about? Did this rabbi ever meet her? That person in the coffin wasn't her anyway. How could it be? I just saw her last week, and she helped me knit a scarf. Even when mine mysteriously widened, my grandmother patiently pulled out my stitches and said, "You can do it *bubeleh*, let's try again."

The rabbi read a Hebrew prayer. I closed my eyes. This is a nightmare, I thought. Any minute I'll wake up and Grandma Sarah will say, "Mandaleh, you're skinny like a rail. How about a *shtikl* pie?"

When someone really dies, I told myself, it happens just like in the movies or on TV. The person gets shot or has a terrible disease, spends a long time in the hospital dying, and manages lifetime advice and good-byes to all the sobbing loved ones crowded around the deathbed. The patient goes through contortions. Machines buzz. Clergymen comfort the wailing relatives. When the person actually dies, arms dropping down the bed rails, everyone sighs at once.

But that was not how it happened with Grandma Sarah. She was alone. After she didn't answer the phone for several hours when she should have been home, my uncle opened the door and found her lying on her living-room couch, he thought, sleeping. But she was cold and dead.

We got a phone call from my uncle. Then my parents made phone calls. Cousins. Aunts and uncles. Friends from Brooklyn, from Mountainview, from the Old Country. The funeral home. The cemetery. The adults picked out a coffin, picked out clothes for my grandmother, picked out food for sitting *shivah.* The dull busywork of death. Not like in the movies.

At Grandma Sarah's funeral, it was quiet. People were polite. No one moaned or screamed. Two people pulled out a tissue from the crocheted boxes. During the service, the only sound came from one lone granddaughter, sitting in the right front pew, making little coughing sounds. Not like in the movies.

•   •   •

They covered the mirrors with navy-blue sheets, sat on little benches, and wore black, slit-ribboned buttons pinned to their chests like first-prize badges at a state fair. In the kitchen, there was no room for a glass of milk on the long table. The brown Formica surface was jammed with tall fruit baskets, wrapped in squeaky gold cellophane, and round tins of brandy-soaked honey cakes, a few topped with those horrid chunks of green- and red-sweetened preserves. Pressed inside their brown, bready centers were slimy, green nutty things that looked like slivers of olives when the cakes were cut. Virginia set up for *shivah,* for a week of mourning, like any good Jewish daughter-in-law.

On the first day of *shivah,* after we returned from the cemetery and hung our coats in the hall closet, Laura motioned to me, and we snuck into her bedroom, with Michael tagging after us. We closed the door.

"Whew," Laura said. "I couldn't wait to get out of there."

"I know."

"If one more person pinches my cheek, I'll die," Laura said, stopping when she realized that she used a word with death in it.

We sat on Laura's bed. Michael curled up in my lap; and I started to twirl his blond corkscrew curls, while Laura and I gossiped as if we had seen each other the day before.

"Did you see Olga's veil at the funeral?" I asked.

"How could anyone miss it?"

"Did you get a load of those little black velvet doodads?"

"Yeah. She looked like she had a bad case of the measles."

"I thought she had a snotball on her nose."

"A snotball! A snotball!" Michael squealed, jumping on the bed.

"Hold your horses," I said, pulling Michael's blue knitted necktie toward me.

"Mandy, you shouldn't have said that," Laura warned, as her brother started to whinny and neigh.

"Okay, Michael," I said. "Stop horsing around. I'm going to rein you in."

"It's not raaa-ining," Michael said in a horsey voice.

"Can you believe how dumb he is," Laura said, but in a way that made me know she didn't mind her brother that much, at least not as much as she used to. "Okay, Mister Horse, why don't you get out and leave Mandy and me alone for a while?" After much begging and bribing, Michael left the room.

"I'm so happy to see you," I said.

"I know. Me too."

"You look very pretty."

"So do you."

"Really? Come on!"

"I swear, Mandy. I wouldn't say it if I didn't think it was true . . . well, maybe I would, but I *do* mean it."

"I want to ask you so many things, I don't know where to begin. Like about school. About what you did in Mountainview during your month there, if you see your other cousins, who your friends are now, and you know, about boys, too."

"There's not much to tell. School is blah as always, nothing new. The only subject I can stand is art. Mountainview was blah also, without you. Mostly, I hung around with Barbara Siegel."

"Tell me *everything*."

We leaned back on the bolster, and Laura repeated every little silly thing Barbara said and did, and, of course, I promised never to say anything to Barbara about our conversation. I told Laura about my month in the country, which seemed almost the same as hers, leaving out the boy part.

That evening, my aunt allowed me to sleep over. Past midnight, with the nightlight on and Michael safely sleeping on the living-room couch, I tossed around on Michael's bed across the room from Laura. After giving up on falling asleep, I asked in a low voice:

"Laura, are you still up?"

"Yes," she said. "I can't sleep."

"Me neither. Laura, did you meet Denny Moskowitz last summer?"

"Who's he?"

"Barbara's cousin from the Bronx."

"Oh, the one with blond hair?"

"Yeah," I said. "He came up for three weeks last summer, but I think he was there for a few days at the end of your month."

"He was very cute if I remember right."

"Don't tell anyone, but we were going steady."

"Come on!"

"Really," I whispered.

"How can that be already?"

"Well, it's kind of embarrassing because he's a year younger than me. But Steve and Barbara, well you know they liked each other last summer. Then Rhonda and Larry were sort of together, so when Denny came up, there were no girls left except me."

"So, what happened Mandy? You're killing me with suspense."

"One night we went to the camp clubhouse, and Larry put on the record player. "For Your Love" was on, and Larry pushed Denny to ask me to dance. It was too, too much, I almost died. In the beginning, we stood as far away as any two people could when they're dancing. Then Larry got up and turned off the lights. I was petrified that some adult would find us, but Larry said no one came that far up the hill at night."

"Then what?"

"Suddenly, Denny put both arms around me the way Larry was slow dancing with Rhonda. We just danced real tight and sweaty for a long time."

"That's all?"

"Well, Barbara and Steve were making out in the corner. We could hear them smacking and rustling and moaning."

"So, did Denny kiss *you* or not?"

"Well, yeah."

"So, how was it?"

"At first, not so good. His braces scraped at my lips, and he didn't know what to do. I don't think he'd had much experience before."

"Why, did you?"

"I went out with some boys from school," I said. "I'll tell you later. Anyhow, after a while, Denny got better."

"Like how?"

"What do you mean? Haven't you ever kissed a boy? I thought Larry liked you before Rhonda. That's what Barbara told me."

"Well, maybe he did. But I was young and shy, and he only kissed me once, and I turned my head so fast, I don't think he even got my lips."

"There's nothing to it, Laura. You'll see. It'll come naturally."

"Show me. Come over to my bed, please."

"Not now. Someone can walk in any second."

"Everyone's sleeping."

"Look," I said, moving to Laura's bed. There was a block of lamplight coming in from the window. I stretched out my arm, smooth side up. "Just take your lips, get them into a good position, and press. It's easy. See." I kissed my arm with one big, long smack.

"But, how about the wetness? Isn't it yucky? Come on, show me. I can't tell how the lips look, how they move. I always see couples in the movies who roll their heads in a circle, but it seems so funny. Please Mandy, I have to know."

Laura worked on me like crazy; and before we knew it, we were locked in the bathroom. Laura got a tube of her mother's lipstick from the medicine cabinet, and we peeled off a little section of the *shivah* sheet that was taped over the mirror.

"Do you think it's okay to do this?" I asked. "I mean maybe it's against Jewish law."

"Don't be silly. It's an old sheet."

"But we're not supposed to be vain or think of ourselves."

"We're not. We're just practicing for the future." When Laura wanted something, she was as relentless as a lawyer.

Laura opened the lipstick and applied it first to her lips and then to mine, keeping her mouth open the whole time as if she were feeding a baby. Maybe she didn't know about kissing, but she sure knew about makeup.

"Good," she pronounced, "blot just a little. Now, first show me on the mirror."

I pursed my lips, leaned close, and kissed the glass, backing away to see a bright-red imprint in a cloudy circle. Laura copied my moves and planted hers right next to mine. Then we started to kiss the mirror all over, peeling back the *shivah* sheet as we reapplied the lipstick and kissed some more. After several times, we blotted our lips on toilet paper, and stepped back to see a mass of red lips, in every position from closed tight to wide open, and smeared fingerprints over the right section of the mirror.

"We'd better get this off quick," I said, realizing the extent of the damage. We spent the next ten minutes rubbing off the red lip prints and drying off the mirror with towels.

"You know, Mandy, I don't think that was really kissing."

"Why not?"

"It wasn't moving, not like they do in the movies. And, tell me the truth, did Denny French-kiss you?"

"Well, yeah, he did."

"Did?"

"I broke up with him in October."

"Really?" Laura's eyes enlarged as if I reported a date with James Dean. Not only did I have experience in the kissing department, but I had a tragic "past."

"Yes, it wasn't much of a romance. Denny couldn't say anything worth hearing."

"But the kissing part. Can you show me how, Mandy? On me."

"No, I'd feel silly."

"Come on. No one will know. If it makes you feel better, I'll turn out the light. Kiss me like you really did it."

"Okay, come here. But if you tell anyone, I'll kill you."

Laura flicked off the light switch and poked her way, giggling, toward me; and before I knew it, I felt her hot breath on my face. I closed my eyes even though I couldn't see too much except for a line of light under the door from the hall nightlight. Laura's closed lips pressed firmly on mine. I couldn't breathe, but I could smell the sour-sweetness of her mother's Aqua Net hair spray. She started to move her head round and round, pinning me against the door. "Is this right?" she asked, panting.

"Yes," I gasped. "But you don't have to move so fast. More like this." I kissed her in a gentle circle, though my heart beat violently.

"And our mouths?" Laura asked. "Should we open them?"

"I'm not opening my mouth! This is good enough. You can do it the same way with a boy, just with your mouth open."

Someone was rattling the handle and pounding on the door.

"Laura, are you in there?" my aunt Virginia screamed.

We both froze as if the door was wide open and everyone in black was watching us. Laura answered a very muffled, "yes."

"What the hell are you doing in there? I don't even see any light coming through?"

"Nothing, we're coming out."

"We, who's we?"

"I'm in here too, Aunt Virginia. Me, Mandy."

"I never heard such a crackpot thing. What do you two girls have to lock yourselves in the bathroom for in the middle of the night? And with the lights out?"

"Nothing. We didn't think it was allowed. You know, when you're sitting *shivah*, to put the lights on," Laura said.

"Of course, you have to see what you're making, don't you? Now do your business and get the hell out of there and get back to bed before you wake up the whole neighborhood."

Laura turned on the light, and we looked at the mirror. The top corner of the *shivah* sheet kept falling under the weakening glue of the tape, and the mirror was still smeary. We wet the corner of a towel and tried to erase the smudges. Every time we placed the sheet back up and ran our nails along the tape marks, the corner collapsed.

"Let's just leave it," I said. "No one will notice." We wet some toilet paper and rubbed the red off our lips.

"You know," I said, as we were getting ready to open the door, "I'm not sure if that was how you do it. I didn't wear lipstick when I kissed Denny."

"Maybe we can try again later," Laura said. "Next time without lipstick."

• • •

During the first hours that we sat *shivah*, Laura and I became best cousins again. Not that we needed hours; I think, it happened the second we saw each other at my grandmother's funeral.

I had been worried about our mothers—how they would act after their fight, which, from overhearing my father and uncle talk, had something to do with money and the closing of our fathers' factory. Though my mother said it had more to do with my aunt's "insane delusions and suspicions" (which seemed to bother my mother but not my father). As far as I could see, there were no fireworks. When the women passed each other at the funeral, they nodded; and when we came to Laura's from the cemetery, Virginia took my mother's hands and dragged her into the kitchen to show her the food. Maybe it was their way of practicing kissing like Laura and me.

The only words I heard about the subject were my mother's telling my father, "Thank God for Virginia taking her Miltown." When I asked my mother if Virginia was going to some other town, she looked at me like I was nuts, so I dropped the whole thing.

On the second day of *shivah*, Laura's cousins came to visit. As we were all looking through Laura's photo album, I heard the doorbell ringing. We didn't feel like seeing more company, so we stayed in Laura's room until we got hungry. I went to the kitchen for food to bring back to the cousins.

There, the women crowded around the sink and counters, wrapping and banging casseroles and spoons, opening and closing cabinets, shoving their sweaty black sweaters into each other. Someone tapped my back as I was bending, searching the refrigerator.

"Mandaleh?"

For an instant, I thought it was my grandma Sarah, coming back because she just couldn't resist so many women fussing in the kitchen. I turned, tears welling, and said, "Mrs. Coffee," and we hugged. I had forgotten Laura had another grandmother, a grandmother nicknamed for her obsession with Chock Full o' Nuts.

We stood there, huddled together against the cold white refrigerator, not saying anything. I whispered to her: "Coffee, Mrs. Coffee?" and she squeezed my shoulders and said, "Don't mind if I do, Miss *Kibitzer*."

I had last seen Mrs. Coffee when she played gin rummy with Grandma Sarah in August, my month in the country, but it seemed like ages ago. I picked up a china cup from the white linen tablecloth that was spread on the kitchen counter and placed it next to the percolator. As I poured the steamy brown liquid, the past summers flashed by like the shuffling of rummy cards. Laura and I stood out, like a magic trick, faceup and mid-deck, a set of red-suited queens.

Mrs. Coffee took her cup, and I followed her into the living room. We sat on Virginia's plastic slipcovered couch, underneath a large oil painting with a stormy sea-foam scene. The picture would come to life when Virginia switched on the top-attached fluorescent lamp, even though the room wasn't dark enough for indoor lights.

She'd show off her expensive Florentine-gold frame, sculptured with naked angels blowing long horns.

When Grandma Sarah first saw that frame years ago, she said to my mother, "Not only is it ugly, but whoever heard a Jewish woman should have lit-up angels all over!" Sarah, like a lot of relatives, seemed to have special rules for what Jews should or shouldn't do.

I handed Mrs. Coffee a bowl of peanuts from the side table.

"Mrs. Coffee, do you think my father and Uncle Sol will still bring their families to the country every summer?"

"Your grandmother left the houses to her sons, but who knows what will happen."

As if reading my mind, she added, "Your grandma was good at managing her daughters-in-law's arguments."

"And," I said, "she was good at playing gin rummy."

"Mandaleh," she said, "I'm so sorry about your grandmother. You know you were very special to her."

I felt a dam burst inside my chest, but I bit my lips together. It wasn't the time to fall apart, not now when Laura needed me again.

BETRAYAL

The deaths in 1959 began with Grandma Sarah but didn't end with her. This time, on a stormy day in April, we all just about broke. This time it was my uncle Sol.

Sol, my grandmother Sarah's youngest son, the gentle, funny, sweet chubby man whose childhood photo, a boy Shirley Temple with long blond curls, still stood on the dresser in the attic of my father's old room in Mountainview. Sol, Virginia's husband, who talked his wife into sanity. Sol, Michael's beloved daddy; and my best cousin's Laura's father, the man whose love she longed for more than anything in the world (something I knew very well). Sol, my father's younger brother. My uncle . . . Sol.

"I knew he just wasn't himself," my mother said a few hours after the shocking phone call about his death. "He seemed a little yellow and sluggish. But with him, you could never tell. He was always complaining of something or other. We just never paid much attention."

For the first few weeks after Sol died, everyone analyzed his death as if the more they figured it out, the better sense it would make. But to me, all these discussions ever accomplished were to make someone feel like a criminal.

A week before he died, Sol said he had stomach pains and was constipated. My aunt gave him three teaspoons of milk of magnesia and told him to lie down. When that did nothing, Sol went to the family doctor who gave him some medicine and told him to lie down. He wound up at the hospital for tests. He was admitted, and a day later he died. Everyone was confused. My aunt kept saying, "Maybe it was something he ate," and she repeatedly went over Sol's entire menu for the past month.

But it wasn't something he ate. An autopsy found that Sol's heart gave out. Something was wrong with his liver and kidneys. His organs were like those of a ninety-year-old man even though he was forty-four. We should have believed him all those years, all those years when things hurt him, and everyone thought he was just a hypochondriac. The guilt was like quicksand.

While we sat *shivah* at Laura's house, I was in a constant haze as visitors floated in and out. It wasn't like when we sat for Grandma Sarah. Now, no one seemed to care about the food in the kitchen or about covering the mirrors or even about getting up to answer the door. Aunt Virginia kept offering Laura, my sister, me, and even five-year-old Michael, pills to help us feel better. Once my mother caught Virginia handing us a tablet from a tiny brown clear bottle, and she let my aunt have it: "Virginia, what's got into you? Giving pills to children! Are you crazy or something?" Of course, nobody needed to answer that question.

We children hid in Laura's room. I was afraid to leave my cousin. I slept at her house from the day her father died.

Laura started picking at her legs again and spent hours in the bathroom squeezing pimples on her face until they bled. She hadn't washed her beautiful thick russet hair for days, and she pinned it up in greasy sections with black bobby pins. I never saw her cry after the first day. Michael made up for it, sobbing all the time.

"Laura, let me wash your hair," I begged on the fifth day of *shivah*.

"No, I don't care what it looks like."

"Well, it looks like a grease ball. Come on."

"I said, I don't care what it looks like!"

"You'll feel better."

"Mandy, leave me alone already. I said, leave me alone! L.M.A! L.M.A! I wish everyone would just L.M.A!"

It was no use talking to Laura, so I tried my best to get her to draw or play a game, anything to get her mind off herself. She just kept saying, "L.M.A."

I was surprised when Laura asked to see our country neighbor Barbara Siegel. I mentioned this to my mother, who reminded me that Barbara's father had died last summer. At my mother's instigation, Barbara visited on the sixth day. When she walked into my cousin's room, Laura's face lit up for the first time, and she crooned, "Barbara! You came!" They hugged, and Barbara sat on Laura's bed.

"You don't look so good," Barbara said, but not in her usual wishy-washy voice.

"I know, Mandy keeps yelling at me."

"So why don't you do something about it?"

I couldn't believe Barbara could be so bossy. Then I stared at her rosy cheeks, not as full as they used to be, and realized what my mother once said about her was true: she was growing into her looks.

Before long, Barbara was rinsing Laura's hair in the bathroom sink and putting Clearasil on Laura's pimples. Miraculously, she got Laura to sit still long enough on the toilet seat to set her hair in big, fat wire rollers and wrap her head with Virginia's hooded dryer. Barbara brushed out Laura's hair, parted it in the center, and let it fall silky and fluffy on her shoulders. Laura looked like a different girl.

As I stood in the hallway staring at them, the two girls without fathers, making themselves up for the world, I felt like I was watching a movie, watching actresses who resembled people I once knew. I stepped back and walked into the living room, joining my mother on Virginia's plastic-covered couch.

"What are the girls doing?" my mother asked.

"Nothing much," I answered. "Getting prettified, I guess."

"Good, they could use it."

"Where's Daddy?"

"In the kitchen with Virginia going over some financial papers."

"Poor Daddy," I said, knowing that Virginia would be harping over some irrelevant details.

Minutes later, my father lumbered into the room. With his hunched shoulders and a few days' growth on his face, he looked much older than forty-eight. He slumped into the chair and lit a cigar. Nobody spoke. I reached into the candy dish and grabbed a handful of M&Ms, tossing them into the air, moving my open mouth to catch them like they were miniature baseballs. "Look, Daddy, I caught two tan ones in a row," I said. My father, who enjoyed playing this game with me, lay back in the chair, expressionless.

"Daddy?" I said.

There was no answer.

I turned toward the hall. Laura and Barbara were still in the bathroom, giggling in the mirror, examining their eye shadow. How could I let them know? How could I tell them that I belonged in that bathroom with them, belonged in the same room with the two girls who had lost their fathers?

• • •

Two weeks before we were going to the country for the summer, I was at Laura's apartment when Barbara Siegel visited. Laura suggested we play Monopoly and after an hour, I was bored, and Barbara complained that she was hungry. Laura went into the kitchen to get some snacks.

"Mandy, let's play this new game I got," Barbara said while I was replacing the cards and money into the Monopoly box. She rummaged in her pocketbook and took out a small box the size of a deck of cards.

"I'm tired of games," I said. "I'd rather listen to records."

"You have to try new things and let go of the old," she said in a snotty tone.

"Are you Miss Experience?"

"Well, at least I'd appreciate a brand-new house."

"What's that supposed to mean?" I asked.

"You never liked your new house in the country."

"So, big deal. Lots of people hate to move."

"Not only that."

"What?"

"You're too attached to your Brooklyn friend Francine." She twirled a strand of her coppery hair.

"I am not." I slammed shut the Monopoly box.

"You are so. Everyone says so, even Laura."

"What does Laura say?"

"Just what I said. That you're too attached to Francine."

"She never told *me* that."

"Well, she told *me*."

"When?"

"Last summer in the country."

"In front of everyone, she said that?"

"No, we were alone."

"Where?"

"Do you have to know every single detail?"

"Just tell me where!"

"By the rock."

"Which rock?" I felt my heart drop.

"You know the one in the woods behind your house. I think it's the rock you used to go to with Laura."

"Exactly *which* rock are you talking about?"

"The rock, what does it matter? It's just a rock. Laura said you two named it the Big Rock."

"Tell me!"

"Well, you go up a trail, after going under that barbed-wire fence, and then there's a rock Laura called the Sun Rock. Then you go up a ways, and it's right under an oak tree. It's nice and private up there."

"Laura took you *there*?"

"What's the big deal?"

"How many times did you go?"

"Only that time."

Laura returned, and before long, I left. Walking home, I went over everything that Barbara had said. I couldn't believe it, I just couldn't. There must be an explanation. Maybe Laura went to the Big Rock because she wanted to bring back the bows and arrows we'd stored nearby, or maybe she went and Barbara had followed her. That must be it. I told myself to call Laura the first thing in the morning.

• • •

"Barbara told me you took her to our rock," I said to Laura on the phone.

There was no response, but I knew Laura was there because I heard breathing.

"Laura?"

"I heard you, Mandy."

"You took Barbara to the Big Rock?"

"So, what if I did?"

"So, what! How can you say that?"

"What's the big deal anyhow? You can be very dramatic sometimes."

"I wouldn't talk if I were you. Did we or didn't we promise each other as blood cousins that we wouldn't take anyone else to our rock, ever? That it was our rock and nobody else's? I thought that was a sacred pledge."

"Mandy, how old are you?"

"You know perfectly well how old I am."

"Well, in September, you'll be in the ninth grade. You're talking about things we said to each other when we were kids. First of all, how do you expect me to remember all that childhood stuff? Second of all, I didn't think you would still care about it."

"If you didn't think so then why didn't you tell me yourself that you took Barbara?"

"Okay, okay. I know how you hold onto things like that."

"Thanks a lot. Now it's all me. You did nothing wrong?"

"I'm sorry if you're mad. See I apologized. Can't we just forget it?"

I wanted to hang up on Laura, but what could I do? After all, she had apologized; she admitted she was wrong. Or did she? Anyhow, I couldn't think straight. I concentrated on breathing in and out, putting off my feelings until I could be alone with them. In the meantime, I controlled my voice and listened to Laura describe her new art book, Michael's recent haircut, and Virginia's last screaming fit.

"Did you draw anything in your artbook yet?" I asked.

"No, I'm not that interested."

"Why not? You love drawing."

"Oh, I don't know. I'm working on a fashion scrapbook right now."

"What for?"

"I'm following the latest fall styles. Barbara says it's important to be ahead of the trends when you're out in the business world."

"Since when do you listen to her? You have plenty of time. Besides, in high school and college, you don't need to be a fashion plate."

"Maybe I won't go to college. Barbara says she may be a secretary and work in a fancy office."

"Come on! You don't want to be a secretary, of all things."

"But I hate school."

"You know your father wanted you to be a lawyer like he was going to be."

"Why does it matter to you? I'm working on this scrapbook."

"Do what you want," I said. "I don't care what you do."

"Mandy? Are you still mad at me? Come on, you know I didn't mean anything by taking Barbara to our rock."

"It doesn't matter," I said, and hung up after mentioning that I'd see her soon in Mountainview. We would finally be there together, after more than a summer apart. I had looked forward to it for so long that I almost tasted the pine needles I'd suck on as Laura and I sat in the Sun House gazebo, swinging back and forth on the couch, rehashing favorite stories. But now, for the first time in my life, I didn't want to go to the country.

Back in my room, I lay on my bed and closed my eyes. I went over, and over the words we had said to each other sitting on our rock, smearing our fingers in blood; and all those times afterwards, sharing our secrets, promising to keep the rock to ourselves. I simply couldn't believe Laura had broken our blood-cousin pledge, that it didn't mean to her what it meant to me. It just couldn't be.

The more I thought back on those first few weeks after my uncle Sol died, it seemed that Laura had stopped confiding in me, stopped gossiping about Barbara, stopped telling me what was in her innermost heart. Just as my father no longer had a brother, just like he mourned him, I mourned for the Laura I no longer knew. Then it dawned on me like an arrow just pierced through my heart, I'd never again tell Laura anything private. I knew then that I'd lost Laura forever.

Then I cried. I had so much crying inside me, that when I stopped, I was so weak I could barely stand. I felt I'd never be able to cry again.

BETTY ANDERSON GOES STEADY

When my family's car arrived in Brooklyn from the Catskills on a sticky morning on Labor Day of 1960, and my father made a right turn from Flatbush Avenue to Avenue I, I could no longer hold out hope that we would be heading home to my apartment on East 22nd Street where my best friend, Francine, lived. Instead, my father headed for the unattached house with the attic and basement described by my mother, who added the one fact that she thought would get me on board: my sister, Brenda, my cousin Nadine, and I would no longer have to share a room. Six months ago, Nadine's father died in a car accident, and her mother had been dead for more than three years, so it was time, my mother insisted, we get a bigger place. Over the summer, she selected the same layout for the three bedrooms, but in different colors. Each would have a new quilted, flower bedspread and coordinated curtains (mine were purple), plus a matching brown Formica dresser and desk. My friends back home in Flatbush, now getting ready for their first year at Erasmus Hall High School, would kill for such luxury.

Maybe Brenda was eager to have her own room, maybe Nadine wanted to go to a snob school like Midwood, maybe my mother favored the idea of having a backyard (more like a tiny deck), and maybe my father figured he could get lost in a big house, but I was NOT going to like this new place. And the first thing I did inside the corner-lot, brick-and-stucco house was run upstairs and scour the hallway for a spot. Tracing the vertical seam on the faded green-swirl wallpaper, I found a tiny cracked peel, lifted it slightly, and wrote in black ink: "I HATE IT HERE." Then I smoothed back the peel so that nobody would notice.

I longed to return to my tiny two-bedroom apartment, with the first-floor view of the Dennehy living room in the next building, and the courtyard I named the Little Back where I bounced Spalding balls from my bedroom window (I didn't mind sharing my room). I longed to run down the stairs and say hi to Mrs. Teitelbaum, my neighbor, get a coconut pop from the Good Humor man, and meet Francine for a quick gossip on the stoop. I longed for my beloved block like a newly adopted puppy howling for its lost mama.

Worst of all, I couldn't tell anyone how I felt (nothing new for me). I should have been grateful to have my clothes no longer jammed into one-third of a closet, to attend the best high school in Brooklyn. I should have been happy for Nadine. Her parents were dead, and she deserved some happiness.

* * *

As I sat on my new scratchy bedspread, I thought of my favorite television show *Father Knows Best* and mourned its cancellation last May. Why did everything that I cared about have to end? During that final episode, when Kathy Anderson refuses to graduate from high school, the show flashes back to a 1956 episode featuring her older sister, Betty, who was also reluctant to graduate. When Betty rehearses her valedictory speech with Dad listening, her voice is unsteady, filled with emotion. Despite Betty's reassurances that she is fine, Jim Anderson asks, "Are you sure everything's okay?" I can't imagine my father ever asking *me* such a question.

Betty decides to boycott her graduation festivities, which includes the dance that evening and the next day's commencement ceremonies. She can't bear for all her wonderful high-school activities to end, and the only way she can stop this process is to "never let it start." Eventually, Jim Anderson saves the day. He shows Betty a page from his wife's diary, dated on the day after *she* had graduated from high school, expressing her fear of leaving everything she loves. Betty realizes she is not the only one who's felt this fear of change. Betty attends the graduation ceremonies, giving the valedictory speech.

I remembered sobbing when I saw that episode. I could picture feeling such sadness if I were leaving the high school I was supposed to go to, Erasmus. Now that I was going to a different school, I wouldn't feel anything but relief when I graduated from Midwood. That is *if* I graduated.

* * *

That feeling was confirmed on the first morning of school when Nadine and I stood outside Midwood's front steps. I fidgeted with the straps on my schoolbag and tried to make casual conversation with Nadine who turned her head back and forth, not paying attention to a word I said. Watching the students greet each other in false cheer, I saw that Midwood was a cliquey place. A tight group of headbanded, flip-haired girls with circle pins and Peter Pan collars sat on a row of stairs. Standing on the right side, several close-cropped, wide-shouldered football-player types shoved each other in that animal grunting way of sporty boys.

Later, during a break, I identified these boys sprawled long-legged at a cafeteria table spitting paper straws toward the white stalactite ceiling. Throughout the morning, other clusters coalesced: the "smart" kids—short girls with bangs and erect postures and short boys with pimples and cuffed chino pants—lined up in the library; the bouncy boosters (also with flips and circle pins) in blue sweaters with a big white "M" huddled by the lockers; the ponytailed, athletic girls gathered in front of the gym. Even the oddballs with sunken chests, baggy eyes, and straggly hair had their place—at the cafeteria table closest to the exit.

At lunchtime, Nadine and I eased into the cafeteria. For once, I didn't want to leave my cousin's side. Students looked up from their plates and stared. Nadine, 5 feet 9 inches tall and wearing a teased beehive making her even taller, and me, barely five feet with a shaggy short cut that wilted under hair spray, were like those mismatched comic characters, Mutt and Jeff. I scanned the rows, and there seemed to be no empty spaces. We must separate, I thought. Nadine veered toward the boosters while I squeezed between two greasy-haired, pimply-faced boys at the table closest to the exit.

On the third day of school, as I met Nadine outside the entrance to walk home together, I noticed a very pretty girl, with straight, shoulder-length, red hair, descending the steps in our direction. Nadine caught her, too, and squealed, "I can't believe it. That's Deborah Korn." Dropping her book bag, Nadine skipped to the bottom steps. "Debbie, Debbie," she screamed, waving her arms. "Here, look it's me, Nadine."

Sure enough, there was Debbie, a girl from my old neighborhood. Living on East 21st Street, a block from my former tenement apartment building, Debbie also attended the same junior high school. Her parents owned the grocery store on Ditmas Avenue—a block and a half from the passageway called the Arcade, a long, dark tunnel that connected my old dead-end street to the stores on Flatbush Avenue. I used to go to the Korns on Sundays for fresh rolls and the newspaper, embarrassed because Debbie's parents yelled at each other in front of customers.

I hadn't known Debbie well, but I admired her ever since she and her friend Linda walked me home through the Arcade one night as we all came from the Canteen Dance. Although it was out of their way, Debbie said it wasn't; she guessed I was scared to pass through the Arcade alone at night and she was right.

Nadine, on the other hand, had more personal contact with Debbie. Linda and Nadine had the same piano teacher, and they performed in yearly recitals since the first grade. Debbie, a loyal friend of Linda's, had suffered through these recitals and always complimented Nadine as if she were Van Cliburn. But anyone would think that Debbie was Elizabeth Taylor from Nadine's jumping up and down.

"Don't tell me you go to Midwood," Nadine said.

"You too?" Debbie asked, nodding.

"Yeah, we moved over the summer," I said.

"I thought someone told me that," Debbie said. "I also moved last month, to Avenue K."

"How do you like it here?" I asked.

"I hate it. I miss the old neighborhood. And Midwood is even worse than I expected. Everyone's so unfriendly."

I said, "I know exactly what you mean."

"Oh, you two," Nadine interrupted, intertwining her arms through Debbie's and mine. "Now that we have each other, the Midwood girls will take notice."

"Who cares?" I whined. "I'm planning to spend all my free time back on East 22nd Street, anyway."

"You would!" Nadine withdrew her arm from me and draped it around Debbie's shoulders, drawing her nearer. "Well, Debbo, I can see that my cousin still needs her precious Francine. It's you and me against the world."

Debbie didn't say anything but glanced at me with a half-smile. Standing on the corner two blocks away, near Brooklyn College, waiting for the light to change, I tapped Debbie on the back and told her I'd see her the next day. I skipped down the street toward my house just as Nadine was chattering about what she and Debbie should wear to the upcoming booster tryouts.

• • •

I thought of Betty Anderson and her beloved high school when I looked around Midwood, at the popular girls, consoling myself that if I dug deeper, someone on the "inside" like Betty would befriend me. Unlike me, Nadine had a plan of action: to get us to the booster tryouts. I had no intention of being humiliated in front of total strangers. And I had no intention of becoming one of those screaming girls, primping for the clean-cut, Ivy-League types, even if one of them turned out to be Betty Anderson. So, I informed Nadine, "Count me out."

"Everyone who's anyone is a booster," Nadine insisted.

"Good for them. Who wants to be *anyone* anyhow?"

"Ex-cuse me, your royal highness. I know you're entirely too good for them. You can sit in a room all by yourself."

For a week, Nadine worked on me. My mother, Brenda, and even Debbie joined the opposition. "What can you lose?" my mother said. Brenda offered, "It's a good way to get friendly with the girls." And Debbie said, "It might be fun. We'll all three go together."

When Nadine said, "You are just afraid you won't make it," of course I had to go. Nadine knew how to get what she wanted, though I suspected her real motives. Maybe she thought a pretty girl like Debbie would help her get in and a plain girl like me would make her look good.

•   •   •

On the day of the tryouts, we were nervous wrecks. Outside the gym, about twenty-five hopefuls were sitting on a bench in the hallway looking at their watches. As each girl came out after a fifteen-minute interview, she looked the same: like she had to carry a ticking bomb across a bed of hot coals. Of the three of us, Nadine went in first, and when she emerged, she said, "It was a piece of cake." Judging from her blanched cheeks, I assumed the piece of cake was laced with castor oil.

The group was dwindling when someone called Debbie's name. "Oh God," she said, "wish me luck."

"Best, best, best of luck," I said, my throat so dry, I wet my lips to swallow. When she came out, Debbie said," I will never get in."

"Why?"

"One girl asked me a question about basketball. Since I never went to a game, I couldn't give her an answer. What a ditz I am."

"That was only one of the questions," I offered, half-heartedly.

It was my turn. When I opened the door, the gym looked enormous. I walked across the shiny wood floor to the other side by the basketball hoops. There were about fifteen girls, wearing their booster sweaters, and two teachers sitting at a long table.

One of the teachers called my name, and I mumbled "yes."

"Speak up," she shouted.

I repeated "yes," and she said, "You needn't yell. Now please read this." She handed me a sheet of paper with two cheers, and I recited them promptly. Then she pointed to an empty chair in the middle of the table and motioned for me to sit. The girls began the interrogation.

"I see that you just moved here," one girl said.

"Yeah. I was supposed to go to Erasmus."

"Oh, there. I bet you're glad to come here, then."

"Erasmus is a good school."

"I'm sure it is."

"Would you have tried out for boosters there?"

"No."

"No? Why not?"

"I wasn't in the booster crowd."

"What did your crowd do?"

"I don't know. Stuff, I guess."

"Why do you want to be in Midwood's Boosters?"

"Because it's a nice group."

"Is it your kind of crowd?"

"I guess so."

"Well, we'll let you know," one of the teachers said.

Suddenly, I realized that I said all the wrong things. "Well, I hope you give me a chance," I whispered and scurried to the door, hating myself for that last remark.

Debbie and Nadine waited outside the building.

"I'm sure I didn't make it," I said. "I can't believe the stupid stuff I said."

"Me too," Debbie said. "One girl, you know the one with platinum-blonde hair, I think her name is Phyllis, anyway she asked me if my hair is dyed. I was so surprised, I said, 'Of course not, I'd never do that,' not realizing then that the boosters' coach, Mrs. Chapin, has dyed red hair."

"Oh, don't worry about it," I reassured Debbie. "I'm sure nobody noticed. Besides, I think that was a good answer."

Nadine was quiet on the way home, and when I asked about her questions, she claimed she didn't remember them. In math the next day, I talked to Ruby Hellman, a girl from boosters, and she mentioned that Mrs. Chapin asked Nadine if her parents approved of her going for boosters. Nadine's face had paled, and she just nodded. Nobody there knew that her parents were dead.

A week later, a list of the girls chosen for boosters appeared on the bulletin board near the lockers. As soon as a crowd gathered, Nadine, Debbie, and I lingered by the lockers, fussing with our clothes and books. As the kids thinned out, we slunk to the notice, looked up and down the columns for our names, turned around, and walked slowly back to the lockers. None of our names were on the list.

Walking from school, no one talked, except to say a few words like, "what do they know?" and "who cares anyhow?" By the time we got to my house, we were riled up.

"What did you expect, anyway? "Nadine said. "New kids just don't get accepted so soon. You have to know the right people."

"The whole process is so horrible," Debbie said. "All those girls against one new person. It's not fair."

"Well, I'm not letting them get away with it," Nadine said. "You'll see, they'll be sorry."

"Who cares?" I said. "It's not life and death. It's boosters."

• • •

Although I enjoyed the episodes with Betty Anderson in high school, I remembered the one when she attends Junior College and goes steady. This was something I could relate to, recalling when I was going steady with Denny Moskowitz, who was twelve, a year younger than I was. Denny was cute, with blond hair and blue eyes, and when I made out with him in the country day camp clubhouse, our braces hooked, and I had to constantly disengage our wires. It wasn't until we were back in Brooklyn after the end of the summer that he gave me his clunky silver ID bracelet. By then, I saw him once in September to go to a movie on a Friday night, and his bracelet was falling off my wrist, but I still wanted to tell my friends that I was going steady. It lasted a few more weeks, and when I broke up with Denny on a chilly day in October (after I got my braces off), the news of who said what to who was more delicious than the announcement of my *steadyhood*.

With Betty, it was even more ridiculous. She is already in college and can scarcely remember that her new boyfriend's name is Roger. From rules devised by the "in crowd," Roger is rated "acceptable" and so Betty accepts him as her "steady." When Jim says, "How can you go steady with a boy you hardly know?" Betty answers in sheer exasperation, "Father Father, you simply don't understand." And Jim Anderson, just as frustrated, comments to his wife, "I thought she had better sense."

I hated to admit it, but I agreed with "Father."

It turns out that Betty's boyfriend Roger is "real neat." According to Betty, he can dance, is good at history, and has a car, an ID bracelet, and a football letter. "What more can you ask for?" she muses.

Dotty, Betty's friend, explains to Mr. Anderson that there are several types of going steady: by telephone, going steadily, regular steady, going steady and not admitting it, and "going ape" when you are falling in a large way. Betty, it seems, is going "straight steady," which guarantees her a whole year of dates.

At the final scene, the gang goes to the Campus Cellar Malt Shop. Betty listens to Roger and her friends bad-mouth the history teacher, Mr. Beekman, an outspoken critic of the social mores. Betty claims that she just remembered that she has another date. Tossing the ID back at Roger, she says, "You might as well chain someone else up with it."

I was so relieved that Betty came to her senses.

•   •   •

That night, Debbie stayed at my house for dinner. On my mother's list of chores, it was Brenda's turn to make the beds, Nadine's to do the laundry, and mine to cook the meal. Debbie set the table while I placed the baked potatoes in the oven and cut up the string beans. My mother arrived home from work at 6:30 and dinner was almost ready, except for the lamb chops my mother brought from the butcher.

"I'll place them under the broiler," my mother said, barely two seconds into the house. "You girls put the laundry away. "Where is Bill?"

I didn't know where my father was. "He was home when we got here," I said. "He must be upstairs in your room."

"Call your father for dinner," she ordered.

With everyone sitting at the kitchen table, waiting for the meat to finish cooking, my mother got up, grabbed the carpet sweeper from the hall closet and started to push it around the living and dining rooms.

"Must you do that now?" my father asked.

"I can't just sit here in a dirty house. Nobody else would do it if I didn't."

"The house is clean. Leave it."

My mother couldn't stop herself. She marched up and down the frayed-green carpet in neat rows, leaving behind darker green stripes and tackling the lighter, unswept columns with the energy of a power lawnmower.

"Mommy, the meat is ready," I called.

My mother gave a few extra sweeps and joined everyone at the table. We ate in silence until my mother, realizing I had a guest, turned to Debbie and asked, "Do your parents still have the store?"

"No," Debbie said. "They sold it."

"Oh, what are they doing now?"

"Is it your business, Estelle?" my father asked, sarcasm dripping from the sides of his mouth like cigar juice.

"I'm just making conversation."

"It's okay, Mr. Gerber," Debbie said." My mother works as a receptionist for a men's clothing business in the city."

"Oh, that's nice," my mother said. "I used to work for a dress manufacturer myself when I was very young. Remember that, Bill?"

"What you being young or that job?"

"Never mind."

"Don't you like the lamb chops?" my mother asked Debbie, noticing that there was one half eaten and another untouched on her plate.

"Yes, they're very good. I'm just full."

After dinner, Nadine, Debbie, and I went up to Nadine's room. "Thank God, your parents didn't ask us about boosters," Debbie said.

"We didn't tell anyone when the tryouts were, and I hope they forget to ask," I said, knowing they wouldn't remember if we had.

"Nadine, I wish you hadn't pushed those tryouts. It was all your idea," Debbie said.

"You didn't have to insult my aunt," Nadine said to Debbie.

"What do you mean?"

"You could have eaten her lamb chops."

"I was full."

"Well, she thought you didn't like them."

"That's not true," I said. "My mother couldn't care less. She was just trying to have a polite conversation."

"Well, I think you insulted her cooking," Nadine repeated.

Debbie's eyes froze in their sockets. "I'm so sorry," she mumbled. "I mean, I didn't realize."

"You didn't do anything wrong, Debbie. Don't pay any attention to Nadine."

"You insulted my aunt." Nadine's thin lips clenched. "You should go downstairs and apologize if you ever want to eat here again.”

Debbie got off Nadine’s bed and ran down the hall into my room. I followed and stood by the open door, but I didn’t see Debbie. I heard her sobbing through my closet door. Nadine appeared inside my room.

“Nadine, you better apologize. It’s your fault that Debbie’s in my closet crying.”

“It’s her own fault. She’s a baby, anyhow.”

“You’re not making sense. Debbie didn’t insult my mother.”

After several minutes, Nadine banged on the closet door. “Debbie, enough already. Come on out.” There was no answer. “Deb, Debbo, come on, don’t take everything so seriously. I was kidding about my aunt.”

Not getting a response, Nadine left my room and headed downstairs. I heard her talking on the telephone, but I couldn’t make out enough words to identify the person on the other end. It was a short conversation.

Debbie opened the closet door and tiptoed to the middle of the room. Her eyes were red and puffy. “Guess I’ll go home now,” she said. “I’m so embarrassed. I hope your mother isn’t insulted.”

“She wasn’t insulted. This is all in Nadine’s mind. Stay awhile. I’m sorry that Nadine hurt your feelings. Believe me, I know how it feels.”

Debbie stood in front of the mirror above my dresser and combed her hair. I watched from my bed, and she could see my face in the mirror’s reflection. “I’ll bet you do,” she said, “I’ll bet you do.”

Nadine returned. “Oh Debbo,” she said, “listen I hope you didn’t take what I said the wrong way. Any Who, forget the whole thing. I have to plan what we’re going to tell everyone in school about boosters.”

“Tell who what?” I said, angry at myself for taking her bait.

“We can’t tell people that we didn’t make it.”

“Why not? We didn’t.”

At that moment, the phone rang, and Brenda screamed, “Nadine it’s for you.”

“Who is it?” she yelled.

“Someone called Stephanie.”

“Coming,” Nadine shouted. “Tell her I’ll be right there.”

“Stephanie?” I asked. “Stephanie who? Not Stephanie from French class?”

“So, what if it is?” Nadine said, heading out my door.

“Is that who you called before?” I asked as Nadine stormed down the stairs.

“Mind your own beeswax,” she yelled, her voice fading and changing into sweetness and light as she picked up the phone. I closed my door.

"Who's Stephanie?" Debbie asked.

"Oh, that popular girl with the short blonde hair. You know her. She sits in front of me in French."

"Don't tell me *the* Stephanie who's in boosters."

"The very same."

•　•　•

It was no surprise that Stephanie became Nadine's new best friend. Nadine brought her candy bars at lunchtime and invited herself to Stephanie's Friday night sleepover. It was also no surprise that Nadine started to hang out with Stephanie's pals at school. When she was with them, she practically ignored Debbie and me.

Maybe I shouldn't have been surprised when Nadine didn't tell Debbie and me about the extra booster tryouts they held before Thanksgiving, or when Nadine announced that she had made boosters after all. But my biggest surprise happened when Debbie, Nadine, and I went shopping at Macy's on Flatbush Avenue one Saturday, and we ran into my old friend, Joyce Platinsky, the first girl in our old school to make out with a boy. Nadine, of course, was wearing her booster jacket and couldn't wait to tell Joyce about her latest rah-rah cheers.

Joyce, who wasn't impressed, turned to me and asked, "How come you and Debbie aren't wearing booster jackets?"

"Oh," Nadine piped in, "They didn't make boosters. Only I did."

And the funny, sad thing was Nadine really believed this. She somehow forgot that all three of us failed the first time, that she bribed her way into being accepted. For that moment outside Macy's, *I* forgot about Nadine ignoring me at school, and Debbie must have forgotten about my mother's lamb chops. Debbie and I stood there, opposite Joyce Platinsky, with mouths open, watching Nadine make-believe.

At that moment, those episodes of *Father Knows Best* flashed in my mind. Maybe *I* wanted a popular friend like Betty Anderson, or maybe a part of me longed to *be* Betty Anderson, but I realized that Nadine's need was greater than mine. And unlike Betty, when it boiled down to the final scene, Nadine didn't come to her senses.

STRANGERS IN THE NIGHT

My parents brought a surprise for my grandmother Mashie when they arrived on the second Friday night of August. Mashie's third husband, Michel, who lived in Berlin, had sent her a dozen long-stemmed red roses and, wrapped heavily with cardboard, a recording of "La Vie en Rose"—their song. Michel was calling for his wife.

There was my grandmother—somewhere in her 60s (her real age a source of family battles)—her cheeks streaked with finger sweeps of flour from making an apple pie, her thick, mostly black hair pulled back with a red-and-black checkered babushka, dressed in a green-and-yellow flowered *shmatte* housedress, arranging her roses in a big orange glass pitcher that we used for lemonade. She sat and read the card: "To my darling wife, Masha. I count the hours till I see you again. Your husband, Michel."

"Mandaleh, bring me a pencil and paper," Mashie said. She had that watery, mushy look in her eyes. "You'll help me write a telegram."

I sat next to her at the dining-room table and waited for her dictation.

"Okay, Mandaleh, ready?" I nodded. "To the one I shall never forget." I groaned at the soppiness, but once Mashie got going, she was in her own world. "No matter where you'll be, and how you'll be, and who you'll be with, I still belong to you. Remember those three little words: forget me not."

"Gram, this is much too long for a telegram. Maybe you should write a letter."

"No, that takes too long. You can take out some words, and sign it, "Your wife, Masha.""

"Good that you put your name, in case he doesn't remember."

"Don't be such a no-goodnik."

Nadine sat on the couch, which was really a hi-riser that Mashie slept on during the weekends when my parents were in the country. Mashie went back to her baking, and I joined my cousin.

"It's unbelievable," Nadine said.

"What?"

"Grandma Mashie. At her age, being so romantic."

"I know. It *is* something. And can you believe that Michel is fifteen years younger and very handsome?"

"I'd love to see his picture."

Nadine didn't know much about Mashie's life since her mother, Louise, and our grandmother had been in the middle of a long feud. Aunt Louise had strongly disapproved of her mother's choice in men (especially Michel) and thought Mashie would be a bad influence on Nadine. Now that Nadine's parents were dead and she lived with my family, she was learning more about our colorful grandmother, and I was the one to spread the word. As Mashie said on many occasions, I was the only young person she knew who was interested in older people. Why that was, I couldn't say except that I must have been born with an extra nosy gene—and I loved my grandmother to death.

I opened the coffee-table drawer and underneath a bunch of pictures of Brenda and me was a photo of Mashie and Michel on their wedding day in 1950. Mashie was wearing a simple dress, hidden by a bouquet of long-stemmed roses, and a hat with a lace veil. One of her arms, wrapped in elbow-length, lace gloves, rested confidently on Michel's shoulder. Her other arm hugged the bouquet while her hand clasped Michel's. She stared directly at the camera. Michel, on Mashie's right, was wearing a tuxedo and looked like a movie star. His eyes focused to his right side, away from his new wife.

"With that mustache, he looks like David Niven," Nadine said. "And with that cleft, a little Kirk Douglas."

"Mashie says he can be as charming as Cary Grant. And when he's on stage at his cabarets, he acts like P.T. Barnum."

"It's funny, I know she's older," Nadine whispered, pushing back the rim on her red, cat eyeglasses, "but they look about the same age."

"He must have been about forty there. The wedding took place in Tel Aviv where they met," I said. My ponytail loosened and I refastened the rubber band with an extra loop. "He had gone to Palestine, it was called then, after the war and opened up a nightclub there."

"How come he never came to America?" Nadine asked.

"I don't know for sure."

"What are you two giggling about?" Mashie asked, ambling to the couch, wiping her hands on a rag. "Oh, you're looking at our picture." Her face was beaming.

"Why couldn't Michel come to this country?" I asked.

"Till today, I don't know. I went to all the big shots at the State Department, and they said, 'We're awfully sorry. It's your husband. Go and ask him. Let him tell you why.' "

"Did you?"

"He said he didn't know."

"Maybe it's because of something he did in the war," my mother said, walking into the room. Cradling a basket of laundry against her large breasts, she was about to go to the main house basement where there was an old wringing washing machine.

"What he did?" Mashie said. "He was in a concentration camp, that's enough. They should be kissing his behind for all he went through."

"Did he ever tell you what happened in the camp?" I asked.

"He couldn't talk to me even a minute."

"That's why he went to Germany," I said to Nadine. "To collect wartime money from the government."

"As if anyone could be compensated for being in a concentration camp," my mother said. "Who knows," she added, "maybe it has something to do with the people he does business with, in Berlin."

"He can't help who comes to his clubs," Mashie said. "And Michel can't help the kind of person he is. He talks to everyone. He don't care who it is."

My mother shook her head as if she had heard this too many times and pushed out the front screen door.

I didn't tell Nadine about the family gossip I had heard over the years. That maybe Michel couldn't get a visa because, according to my aunt Ruthie, he was a Russian colonel; or, according to my uncle Jack, he worked for Israeli intelligence; or, according to my uncle Irving, his shows had *faygelahs* in women's clothes. My mother used to say when she was feeling more sympathetic toward Michel, "You have to remember the times. He not only had ex-Nazis for customers, but most of his family still lives in Russia. With such ties, he could have been an innocent victim of paranoid McCarthyism."

•   •   •

By Sunday, Mashie had her hair cut, nails polished, cuticles trimmed, good slacks ironed, and diamond ring buffed. She was ready for Germany. That night, before they left, we heard on the radio that the East Germans had built a wall separating them from West Berlin to stop the flow of refugees pouring into the West. Michel must have known something.

Nothing now could keep Mashie away, even the protests of my mother, who, agreeing with Nadine's dead mother, suspected that Michel had been after Mashie's inheritance from her dead second husband, a wealthy owner of Brooklyn apartments.

And my mother wasn't too happy to take Mashie back to the city and leave Brenda, Nadine, and me on our own for the last two weeks of the summer. Mashie had been our "chaperone" since late June when my mother went back to work and commuted to the country with my father for the weekends. She got a job at a graphics wholesaler; and, as she pointed out on many occasions, she was bookkeeper, receptionist, telephone operator, and coffee maker. She may have complained to us, but I knew she was happy to be "indispensable" and bragged of her new relationship with a local artist, Andy Warhol, who came in to buy silk-screening supplies.

All this meant no adult supervision, but Brenda was very convincing, pointing out that she was nineteen and a college student and could certainly handle two fifteen-year-olds and any petty problems we had. Besides, there was the telephone and Aunt Virginia, a shout away in the main house with her two children. I was sad to say good-bye to Mashie, but the second my father's car pulled out of the driveway, we couldn't contain ourselves.

"Freedom!" Brenda shouted.

Nadine and I hugged and jumped. This was the closest I had felt toward her since we both got braces on the same day four years ago. We walked in the house, arm in arm, bursting with excitement.

"Let's raid the refrigerator," I said.

Brenda ran into the bedroom for something and zoomed back into the living room with a pack of Winstons and an ashtray. She lay on the couch, positioned a throw pillow under her Natalie Wood flip, grabbed some magazines from the table, lit a cigarette, and inhaled deeply. "Ah, this is the life," she said. "Mandy, how about bringing me some potato chips?"

"Get them yourself. Don't think you can boss me around now."

"You'd better watch out because I'm the oldest person in this house."

"Let's call Elliot and invite him over with the other kids," Nadine said.

"Wait, before we have boys here, let's make sure that eagle eye doesn't find out. The last thing we need is Aunt Virginia calling up my mother and squealing on us," Brenda said.

I looked out the window down the sloping lawn toward the main house. The curtains fluttered in Virginia's kitchen window. "She's spying already," I said. "I bet she even has binoculars." From her recent phone call to ask if we needed anything, I learned that my cousins Laura and Michael had gone to the bungalow colony's concession to buy groceries. Without her children's criticism to stop her, Aunt Virginia could watch us to her heart's content.

I paced the room, which was divided into a kitchen, dining alcove, and living area. "Hey, maybe we could get Laura to keep her busy when the boys come. Or I know," I added, feeling incredibly creative, "they could sneak through the back-bedroom windows. She'll never see."

"What if she decides to pay us a surprise visit?" Brenda said. "Let's just keep it quiet the first night."

But word spread and by Monday night, two waiters at the Shady Grove Hotel, Elliot and Stuart, and later, two town boys, Danny and Jerry, crawled through the windows. Our neighbor Barbara Siegel and her cousin Wendy came through the front door. How could my aunt object to a few girls? Brenda was staying late at Shady Grove, so we had the house to ourselves. We turned off most of the lights, put on the radio, and Jerry passed his pack of Camels. We leaned back on the couch inhaling our lungs out.

On Tuesday, Wendy showed up and told me there was company at the back window. There were Rick and Paul, busboys from the Hillcrest Hotel, a few miles down our road. Wendy and I locked ourselves in the bedroom with the boys, slurping, and lip-squeaking to the night sounds of crickets and tree-breeze swooshing in the woods. Nadine was on the living-room couch with Elliot, and Barbara and Stuart were in my parents' bedroom. Brenda was likely with her new boyfriend, the waiter Kenny, in his room at Shady Grove. We heard that the townies were with girls at Mountainview Day Camp where Nadine and I were counselors. That night, it seemed that everyone I knew was making out in some corner of the Catskills.

* * *

At about 10 p.m., even with our bedroom door closed, I could hear pounding on the front door. "Oh my God, someone's knocking," I said, jerking up and straightening my clothes.

"Relax," Rick said. "It's probably one of the kids."

"But they know to come to the back windows first. Quick, Wendy, get up. Someone's here." I turned on the light and motioned for the boys to get out the window. I opened the other bedroom door and whispered that Stuart had to go. The lights were out in the living room, but I could see the dark figures of Nadine and Elliot. "Elliot's leaving," Nadine said, pushing him toward the bedroom. Before I could do anything else, the front door opened. It was my Aunt Virginia.

"What's going on in here?" she said. "It's a good thing your mother gave me an extra key. Why didn't you answer the door?"

"We didn't hear anything. We were in the bedroom."

"And why are the lights out?" she asked, turning on the lamp by the door as I pushed the ashtray under the couch. "What's that noise?" There was a clunking sound coming from the boys slamming the wooden frame of the bedroom window screens. I shrugged. "And what is that smell? Have you girls been smoking again?"

Just then, my cousin Laura walked inside. "See I told you everything was okay," she said to her mother.

"Maybe *you* think so. Smoking, and who knows what else was going on here. I'm going to call your parents, Mandy. Where is Brenda anyway? I thought she's supposed to keep an eye on you."

"She just went to Shady Grove for a while."

"And left you girls alone?"

"What's going to happen to us?"

"It's what's already happened. I'm calling Shady Grove, too. Laura, hand me the phone."

We all sat still while Virginia had Brenda paged and waited at least ten minutes for her to get on the phone. "Where the hell are you, Brenda? Get home now."

Then she slammed the phone down and called my house in Brooklyn. By now, she was panting, and her voice was high and creaky as if on the verge of her hysterical fits: "Estelle, Virginia. What's wrong? What isn't wrong! I told you a hundred times not to leave the girls without adult supervision. Well, first I heard scurrying in the back. I wouldn't be surprised if boys were here. Brenda left the girls alone. Yes, Brenda, your precious eldest. So, when I came in, the lights were out, and I could smell smoking. Wendy and Barbara are here. Wendy's lipstick is all smeared, and Barbara's blouse is coming out of her pants. Mandy and Nadine look dazed, too. It's a regular orgy. What kind of mother are you leaving them like this? Mandy, here's your mother." Virginia threw the receiver on the couch.

I took the phone and listened to my mother say we should behave, that she didn't need another phone call from Virginia of all people. Then Brenda flew in the door, screaming, "What the hell is going on here?"

"Nothing," Nadine said. "We didn't do anything. But Virginia doesn't believe us."

"Believe you! Why should I? They think I'm a total idiot. I know what happens with boys. Listen Brenda, your mother doesn't want to send the girls to my house. Okay, if she wants to give you her blessing, what do you expect? But Laura will not be allowed to step foot in this house again."

"Mother!" Laura shrieked. "I hate you. I'll do what the hell I want. Who do you think you are anyhow?"

"I'm going to brain you, you lousy kid."

Laura ran out the door with Virginia following. I could hear Virginia yelling in that thin, scratchy wail of hers, like the inhuman sounds that came out of Mashie when she had a nightmare and then insisted the next morning that she didn't sleep the whole night. Barbara and Wendy left quietly, and Nadine, Brenda, and I silently went around the house, picking up dishes, emptying ashtrays, and putting clothes in the hamper. This was the first time I could remember that we three girls didn't fight about cleaning up.

• • •

The next night, we decided to lay low. Brenda, Nadine, and I ate macaroni and cheese, read magazines, played hearts, and went to bed. In the middle of the night, I got up to go to the bathroom and heard a car motor revving in the distance. I raced into the living room and looked out the window. In the darkness, I could make out the swaying branches of a linden tree. I couldn't see the moon, but I knew it was a sliver since I had walked to Aunt Virginia's earlier in the night to borrow ketchup for a late-night french fries snack and, on the way back, almost banged into an Adirondack chair in the middle of the lawn.

I was about to turn toward my bedroom when the motor noise got louder, and misty headlight beams became wider and shorter until the terrace was awash in light. "Somebody's here," I screamed. "Brenda, Nadine, wake up! There's a car in the driveway. Hurry." Then I added, "Don't turn on the light." Somehow, I sensed that we should keep our presence unknown.

The girls came out of the bedroom rubbing their eyes, and we huddled by the door, looking out the living-room window at a dark Cadillac we had never seen before. Suddenly, everything went black as the car motor was turned off, but we could see shadowy shapes moving closer to our door.

"Brenda, they're coming here. Oh my God," I gasped, my heart galloping.

"Who can they be?" Nadine said, her voice rising in panic.

"Hurry, Nadine, make sure the back door is locked," Brenda said. "Mandy, go lock the windows in the bedrooms."

We returned to the living room and glommed together as a unit. By now, Nadine, who held in her emotions when her mother and then her father died, seemed to shrink seven inches to my now-growing five-foot-two. On my other side, Brenda was as rigid as a rifle, and I was shaking so hard it was good that I was pressed in the middle. The clumps of heavy shoe beats traveled from the cement driveway across the walkway and up the steps to our terrace.

"Should we call someone?" I asked. "The police?" It seemed that the kitchen wall phone was a mile away. I heard the screen door open and a fumbling, jangling sound. I stopped breathing.

The door burst open and Brenda screamed, "Who is it?"

"Shh, it's okay," a man said, shining a flashlight at us. I could see four big men, wearing hunting caps and plaid flannel shirts, too warm attire for August. Behind them, someone was rustling something. The men were so tall, they blocked my view, and the flashlight spotted my eyes and went off, not before I had briefly caught the silhouette of a shorter man's back as he staggered down the hall toward the bathroom. I heard him shuffle into my parents' room and slam the bedroom door.

A horrible liquor, tobacco smell was coming from the men. Nadine grabbed my hand and Brenda said, "Who are you? How did you get our key?"

One of the men said, "Go to sleep, we'll be outta here in a jiffy."

Another man with a high-pitched voice asked if we had any beer. Someone poked me in the back. The man squealed, "Yeah, you." Somehow my feet took me toward the refrigerator, an instant of flashlight beam leading me. I grabbed three bottles and, in darkness again, handed them to one of the bodies who stretched out his arm.

I could hear the drunk man leave my parents' room and plod toward the bathroom. All his movements were echoed in the living-room silence. There was the thudding of the squeaky toilet seat cover, and then the gurgling and bursting of the loudest and longest pee I had ever heard. He didn't even close the door. Then, there was a clearing-throat sound and choking, and I realized the man was vomiting.

"Hey, you okay?" the man with the flashlight called. His flashlight started to blink and then go off. He banged it on the wall. Everything went dark, except for the darker shades of moving bodies. "You okay?" the man repeated.

A weak voice said "yeah."

Brenda, Nadine, and I stood frozen, maybe ten feet from the men, waiting for the one who was throwing up to finish. By now, Brenda was hysterically crying, and Nadine and I were heaving into each other like an accordion.

I could now smell vomit mingling with alcohol and heard the drunkard teetering down the hall. From flickering glimpses, I saw the outline of his hunched back sneaking toward the door.

"Ready?" the man with the flashlight said.

Brenda began to shake on my right side, and I was afraid that I would vomit next.

He kept flicking the flashlight switch, and a beam shone in our direction. "Go to bed now. Pretend we were never here." Then he flashed the light on the door, and Brenda and I let out a gasp. The shorter man was my father.

"Get that damn thing outta my eye," my father slurred. The men stumbled outside, and I watched the car back down the driveway, its lights getting thinner and longer.

"Oh God, I can't believe that was Daddy," Brenda said, her voice ragged with phlegm.

I was about to agree, but when I opened my mouth to speak, a torrent of tears came out, as loud as my father's urine stream.

"Oh Mandy, it's okay, they're gone." As Brenda said this, she kept looking out the window. "What was he doing here?" she said, straining her neck into the darkness. "And at this hour? And drunk like that?"

Nadine straightened up to her height and said, "And who were those men? They looked so mean."

That was all the conversation we could muster. We then stood there, no one having the nerve to respond. I checked my parents' bedroom and found the drawer to a small desk near my father's side of the bed overturned on the floor. Underneath, there were loose papers, most of them from the bank or lawyers about the ownership of the house. I placed them into the drawer and slipped the drawer back into its grooves. Then I got a mop out from the closet and walked to the bathroom to clean up my father's piss and vomit.

•　　•　　•

We pushed our three beds together and left the light on. Eventually, I heard Nadine's heavy breathing. I pulled the blanket over my head but heard shuffling noises and sat up with a start. Brenda was not in her bed. I found her glued to the living-room window, peering at the driveway.

"Did you see anything?" I asked.

"No."

"Come back to bed."

"You go, Mandy. I'll be right there."

"Who do you think those other men were?" I asked.

"I have no idea. At first, when I saw the Cadillac, I thought it might have been Leon. Do you remember him? Daddy's old friend? He had a Cadillac."

"Of course, I remember him." The name alone felt like a bomb exploding in my stomach.

"Mandy, I never told this to anyone before, but Leon once made a pass at me."

I could barely respond. "Oh, no," I eked, adding, "when?"

"It was the last summer he stayed at Shady Grove. Four years ago, when I was a counselor there."

I slid, my back hugging the front door. I struggled to breathe.

"What, Mandy? Are you shocked?"

"No. Can I ask you what happened?"

"I was taking the campers back to the main house for lunch. We had been swimming, and I was still in my bathing suit. I was on my way home to change, and he snuck up behind me when I got to Ratner's. He stopped me by the laundry room and asked me to come inside for a second. He had something to show me. I must have been totally dumb, and I followed him inside. He pushed me against the washing machine and tried to kiss me. I can still feel his slobbering lips."

"Oh my god. Then what?

"I kicked him in his balls and ran out. What did he think I was, a complete idiot? I mean who would ever let that creep touch you? Even his wife must have to close her eyes and dream of Rock Hudson."

"That's terrible," I said.

"Anyhow I don't even like to think about him."

"Brenda, can I ask you one more thing?"

"Of course."

"Did you ever tell anyone, you know about Leon?"

"No Mandy, I couldn't. I don't know why, but I felt guilty like maybe I shouldn't have been wearing my bathing suit without a cover-up. I didn't think our parents would believe me anyway. They always think I'm boy crazy, and they adore Leon. Why? I can't imagine."

Then Brenda squatted to the floor and said, "And, Mandy, you're the only one I told."

"Thanks for trusting me. I won't tell anyone." She had no idea that I was an expert in keeping secrets.

Brenda didn't say more. A warmth overcame me that my sister had confided in me, and me alone. For a second, I thought of confessing to my sister about what I did with Leon, but remembered her words, "Who would ever let that creep touch you?" Then, enormous cramps clutched my abdomen, and I felt my entire insides heaving for release. I ran to the bathroom but kept the door open.

On Friday night, my father's car drove up the driveway. My mother was not the only woman to get out. "Girls make way for your grandma. I need the toilet free." And there was Grandma Mashie, back in her country shorts and sleeveless, V-neck blouse.

"Why is Mashie here?" I asked my mother as my grandmother dashed to the bathroom.

"After Virginia's frantic call, I asked Mashie to postpone her trip to Berlin for a week. So, you girls will only have one week unchaperoned."

"No," I said, "Michel will be so disappointed."

"Actually, he said he had to go to Russia for a few days anyhow."

"Why? Is someone in his family sick?"

"Your grandmother asked him, but he said it had to do with business. What kind, he didn't say."

"Another Michel mystery."

"Men! Who can understand them?"

My father plopped on the couch and asked me to get him a beer. Before long, he was reading the sports page of the newspaper.

"How is the city? Did you see any of my friends?" I asked as if I hadn't seen him two nights ago. He grunted an answer and let out a loud gurgling belch. I had no way of knowing if he remembered he had thrown up in the same bathroom now being used by his mother-in-law.

•   •   •

After my parents left that Sunday night, Brenda and Nadine went to Virginia's to play Monopoly with Laura. I pretended I had cramps; I was expecting my period any day, so it wasn't a total lie. I didn't want to see my aunt for even a minute. I sensed that she must have seen something about that night with the men; though in my heart, I knew that if she had, she would have called the police and we would have been hauled to a juvenile detention center for abandoned teenagers.

Sitting at the dining-room table, Mashie took out a deck of cards and cut it in half, tapping each on the table to smooth out the edges. Then she shuffled the deck, and most of the cards flew out of her hands, landing on the linoleum floor. No matter how she tried to neaten them, she didn't have a tight grip. It wasn't in her nature to be controlled. I gathered the cards together and handed them to her.

"Sit," she said. "Play a little gin rummy with your grandmother."

"I don't know."

Normally, I would be thrilled to play cards with Mashie, to have no one else around. But I just couldn't shake this feeling of dread, that any second, those men would return, and I should somehow be prepared. I was thinking of getting the baseball bat from the garage and placing it inside the umbrella stand by the door, when Mashie, said, "Mandaleh, sit down, you're acting like a dog without a bone."

"Okay, Gram, I'll play, but just one game."

After discarding a few cards back and forth between us, Mashie said, "So, Mandaleh, what is wrong a grandmother can't fix?"

"Nothing."

"You can fool some people, but I wasn't born yesterday."

"But close to it."

"There's a Yiddish expression my mother used to say, 'If you want to avoid old age, hang yourself when you're young.' "

"Oh, Gram."

"She also said, 'Better pour out your troubles to a stone, but don't carry them in yourself.' "

"There's a Jewish expression for everything."

"*Nu?*"

"Okay, I was just wondering if Mommy mentioned anything about Daddy this past week."

"She talks about him, so what?" Mashie threw out a queen of hearts, and I picked it up.

"Well, did she mention that he didn't come home one night?"

"Why do you ask such a question?"

I laid the cards on the table.

"Do you have gin already?" Mashie asked.

"No, I just wanted to tell you that Daddy came up here on Wednesday night." I thought I was going to faint right there, flopping my head on the three queens.

"What do you mean?"

I told my grandmother the entire story, and for once, she didn't interrupt. When I finished, she took a cigarette from her pack of Parliaments and inhaled heavily, the smoke curling into her long, narrow nostrils. As she exhaled, she said, "The *mamzer,* the bastard."

When I mentioned the papers in the desk drawer, she said, "The deed! Did he gamble it away? Oh my God, the *mamzer,* the *mamzer.*"

"You have to promise me, Gram, that you won't tell Mommy."

"Why? She should know."

"She will just get upset and yell at him and make things worse. Please, Gram, you have to promise."

"I promise," she said, in a non-Mashie, soft voice.

We played a few more games, throwing out cards without looking at our hands. We each let the other win. I went to sleep early, and Mashie came into the room and sat on my bed.

"Mandaleh, you're a big girl now. You know things go on between adults that make no sense."

"Don't tell me your mother had an expression for this."

"She used to say, 'At night, all cows are black.' "

"And in the morning?"

"Maybe some of the cows have spots."

• • • •

Two days passed and Mashie and I didn't discuss my father again. The next day when I came home from my job as a counselor, I heard her talking on the phone. She hung up shortly after I opened the refrigerator and got a Coke.

"Who was that?" I asked.

"Oh, just a busybody."

"Was that my mother?"

"Okay Miss Detective, yes it was. She was leaving her office, and she couldn't talk. But she says hello."

"Did you tell her about the men coming to the house?" By now, I was yelling.

"Don't have a fit. We didn't talk about it."

I didn't believe her.

When my parents came that weekend, and it was time for them to take Mashie with them back to the city, and my father was putting the bags in the trunk, my grandmother took me aside and smothered me in a big hug. "Don't worry so much, Mandaleh," she said. "Everything will be as it should be." With that, she looked at my mother with her eyes pinched.

"Yes, don't worry, Mandy," my mother said. "I have to take care of a few things in the city, but I will be back by Wednesday. I'm taking the bus."

At that moment, I knew my grandmother had broken her promise to me. I also suspected that this would be our final summer in the country.

•　　•　　•

The last week of August went quickly. Mountainview Day Camp held a fair, and I was chosen to be one of the counselors to stand on a ladder and have buckets of water released on my head if someone was lucky enough to hit me three times in the face with a beanbag. I got five- and ten-dollar tips from all the campers' mothers, everyone that is but the mother of the monstrous hitter and biter, six-year-old Chucky Diamond. Wouldn't you know that the family of the one giving me the most trouble would show the least appreciation? But I did receive satisfaction from Chucky when I went to hug him good-bye, and he started to cry.

At the Hillcrest Hotel, we said good-bye to the boys who worked in the kitchen. Rick promised to call when we got back to the city. He lived in Queens, which seemed as far from my house in Brooklyn's Midwood section as Mountainview.

Another bouquet of roses came for Mashie. Apparently, Michel got mixed up and thought Mashie was still in Mountainview instead of lounging on a deck chair and dining with the Captain aboard the *Queen Mary*, on her long journey that would take her to Germany. Although I missed my grandmother terribly, I was still angry at her. Would I ever be able to snuggle with her and listen to her stories of smuggled jewelry at border crossings, and female impersonators in Michel's cabaret? Would she ever become my darling grandma again?

There was a terrible storm on Wednesday so my mother couldn't come up on the bus. But she sent Virginia to check on us, which she did on an hourly basis. And, my mother called several times in between. Once she asked me to look through my clothes in the closet and decide what I wanted to throw out. When I asked why, she just said, "Because I said so." I didn't want to believe what I dreaded: that we weren't coming back next summer, or ever. But my mother did give me one certainty. During each conversation, she made sure I knew that my father was safely in the Brooklyn apartment.

We kept the house quiet that week, except for one big spaghetti dinner for our friends from the bungalow colonies, which lasted until nine o'clock, when we practically kicked them out of the house. We invited no one else, secretly afraid of another surprise visit from the men in the dark Cadillac. It was a kind of silent agreement between us. As far as that actual night was concerned, Brenda, Nadine, and I never spoke of it again.

AUTHOR'S NOTE

When I began writing creative fiction and nonfiction close to thirty years ago, childhood memories emerged, poking through the debris of structural guidelines and exercise prompts. The more I tried to fashion these images into recognizable forms, the more they resisted strictures. Eventually, they became stream-of-consciousness ramblings, character sketches, and expanded into short stories and personal narratives. Over the years, I added new stories and revised the old. Some evolved into close recreations of memories; others became embellished or changed into totally invented scenes.

Some characters owed their inspiration to real people; some were complete fabrications; and others began as familiar models and morphed into combined semblances. As an homage, I kept the real names of my two grandmothers (Masha and Sarah) and a husband of one (Michel); other characters took on names and physical traits of their own. The name of the Catskill village was changed; yet the name of the Brooklyn streets and schools remained the same as my own. Certainly, determined sleuths could unearth geographical and character markers, but they would be hard-pressed to make a full case for absolute replication.

I apologize to anyone who feels offended by personal similarities. I hope that the portrayals and events in this book are judged or enjoyed by their literary merits. Whether fiction or nonfiction, the essence behind each story is my own unassailable truth.

ACKNOWLEDGMENTS

During the decades of writing this book, it has gone through numerous iterations (and names). It succumbed to long slumbers, where it languished in my desk drawer, until it came to its final resting place as a novel-in-stories. Along this journey, I have had many loyal readers and helpmates: from Barbara Packer, when we talked endlessly about the initial story during that magical week at the lake, and who more recently drove me to the Neversink and the famous Croton Bridge; to my Madeleine L'Engle-inspired writing group and network, who met for over twenty-five years and continues to nurture; to my MFA City College fellow students and professors, who inspired new stories and gave me great suggestions for improving old ones.

Even before *Floating in the Neversink* was the germ of an idea, there were two people who not only provided the inspiration for the character of Francine but encouraged me to make up stories when we were children. Thanks to Joan Audrey Schneider Katz and Carol Helene Schneider Schweid for being my fearless partners in the Adventures of the Super Triplets of Flatbush.

The list of encouraging relatives is also long. Many have offered their stories, interpretations of events, and even their personalities (wittingly and not) as fodder for my imagination, understanding that the business of a writer often means mysteriously mishmashing the real and the imagined. The family member who knows me the longest is my sister, Barbara Simon Hoffmann, who has always encouraged me to tell my own truth even if it differs from hers. She is the one who reminded me, during a moment of familial anxiety, of the Benjamin Franklin quote: "If all Printers were determin'd not to print any thing till they were sure it would offend no body, there would be very little printed."

And, of course, when it comes to my family, profound thanks to the two people who have shown unfailing love and support, and for accompanying me to the Catskills: my daughter, Alexis Zoe Simon Neophytides, and my husband, Andreas Neophytides.

Special thanks to Michelle Cameron for her astute and compassionate editorial comments that greatly improved the emotional quality and cohesiveness of this book, and for recently re-reading it. Thanks to Michele Menzies-Abrash for the Catskills postcards and for another reading, and to dear friend and writing buddy Katherine Kirkpatrick, who helped me refashion the book's beginning and commented on the manuscript. Other inspired readers include: Stephanie Cowell, Helene Ebenstein, Penny Laitin, Pamela Leggett, Alexis Neophytides, and Kay Sloves whose loving and astute comments and support were essential.

For tireless and comprehensive encouragement, thanks to Rachel Tarlow Gul of Over the River Public Relations. At Black Rose Writing, I am extremely grateful to Reagan Rothe, publisher, for giving the book "life" and for patiently attending to my numerous e-mails; and to David King, design director, for his responsive input. A special thanks to Kevin Beard for translating my cover ideas into the most compelling design.

AUTHOR'S BIO

Andrea Simon is a writer and photographer based in New York City. For the past several years, she has devoted her efforts to fiction and literary nonfiction, including her published memoir/history, *Bashert: A Granddaughter's Holocaust Quest,* now in paperback, and her award-winning historical novel, *Esfir Is Alive.* Andrea has published numerous stories and essays and has received prestigious literary honors. She holds an MFA in Creative Writing from the City College of New York where she has taught writing.

FROM THE AUTHOR

Word of mouth is crucial for any author to succeed. If you enjoyed the book, please leave a review online—anywhere you are able. Even if it's just a sentence or two. It would make all the difference and would be very much appreciated.

Thanks!
Andrea

Thank you so much for reading one of our **Literary Fiction** novels.

If you enjoyed our book, please check out our recommended title for your next great read!

The Five Wishes by Mr. Murray McBride by Joe Siple

2018 Maxy Award "Book of the Year"
2018 PenCraft Award 1st Place "Fiction-Drama"
2018 American Fiction Awards Finalist
2018 ScreenCraft Cinematic Book Award Finalist
2018 Wishing Shelf Award (UK) Finalist

"A sweet...tale of human connection...will feel familiar to fans of Hallmark movies." –*KIRKUS REVIEWS*

"An emotional story that will leave readers meditating on the life-saving magic of kindness." –*Indie Reader*

View other Black Rose Writing titles at
www.blackrosewriting.com/books and use promo code **PRINT** to receive a **20% discount** when purchasing..